4/10

TEEN

THE OTHER SIDE OF
BLUE

THE OTHER SIDE OF
BLUE

by Valerie O. Patterson

CLARION BOOKS
Houghton Mifflin Harcourt
Boston   New York
2009

Clarion Books
215 Park Avenue South, New York, New York 10003
Copyright © 2009 by Valerie O. Patterson

The text was set in Deepdene H.
Map by Tom Patterson.

Clarion Books is an imprint of
Houghton Mifflin Harcourt Publishing Company.

www.hmhbooks.com

Printed in the United States of America

Library of Congress Cataloging-in-Publication Data

Patterson, Valerie O.
The other side of blue / by Valerie O. Patterson.
p. cm.
Summary: The summer after her father drowned off the island of Curaçao,
Cyan and her mother, a painter, return to the house they stay at every summer,
along with the daughter of her mother's fiancé, but Cyan blames her mother
and spends her time trying to find out what really happened to her father.
ISBN 978-0-547-24436-5
[1. Mothers and daughters—Fiction. 2. Grief—Fiction. 3. Artists—Fiction.
4. Stepsisters—Fiction. 5. Secrets—Fiction. 6. Curaçao (Netherlands Antilles)—Fiction.] I. Title.

PZ7.P278152Ot 2009
[Fic]—dc22
2008049233
MP 10 9 8 7 6 5 4 3 2 1

Dedicated to
Tom
And to our nieces
Nicole, Leah, Emily
Annie and Patty
With love
and hope

ISLAND OF CURAÇAO
Netherlands Antilles

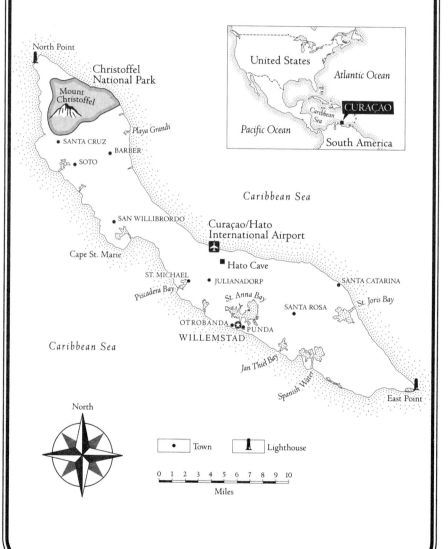

North Point

Christoffel
National Park

Mount
Christoffel

Playa Grandi

• SANTA CRUZ   BARBER

• SOTO

SAN WILLIBRORDO

Cape St. Marie

Caribbean Sea

Curaçao/Hato
International Airport

Hato Cave

ST. MICHAEL   • JULIANADORP

Piscadera Bay

St. Anna Bay   SANTA CATARINA

OTROBANDA   SANTA ROSA   St. Joris Bay

PUNDA

WILLEMSTAD

Caribbean Sea

Jan Thiel Bay

Spanish Water

East Point

United States

Atlantic Ocean

CURAÇAO

Pacific Ocean

Caribbean
Sea

South America

North

| • | Town | | Lighthouse |

0 1 2 3 4 5 6 7 8 9 10
Miles

"[A] blue surface seems to retire from us. But as we readily follow an agreeable object that flies from us, so we love to contemplate blue, not because it advances to us, but because it draws us after it."

—Johann Wolfgang von Goethe,
Theory of Colors

W E'RE IN PARADISE, so the tourist brochures say. That's what I thought, too, before last June, when the unspeakable happened, when Dad took the blue boat out and didn't come back.

The Caribbean island of Curaçao beckons sun worshipers and cruise ships that sail up St. Anna Bay and dock near the House of the Blue Soul. Taffy pink, aqua, and lemon yellow buildings like squares of colored candies line the streets of Willemstad's shopping district. *Bon bini* signs welcome arrivals at every port of call, the airport, and almost every shop in Punda and Otrobanda. They're even plastered to the side of boats taking tourists out to scuba-dive in deep water. *Paradise.* Where the water is so blue, so calm, so deceptive.

"You're sure you don't want to come with me, Cyan?"

Standing in the driveway outside our rented house, Mother says my name—Cyan—like a sigh. "I'm sure Kammi would appreciate your meeting her at the airport. You know, the first time. To welcome her."

I shake my head while the dry wind billows my broomstick skirt like a sail. The girl in the photograph Mother showed me last night—the one she keeps in her art studio— is younger than I am. Thirteen, Mother said, two years younger. Her face in the photo appears fair and freckled across the nose, but she has brown hair, not blond like me. She's thin, too, not fat. I studied every detail.

Mother opens the car door and folds herself into the back seat of Jinco's rusty faded-denim-colored taxi. Untroubled by the wind, her spiky short hair sets off her sharp cheekbones. Today she's highlighted them with a subtle peach color, but she's still all angles, down to her creased linen pants, bony ankles, and pointy red leather mules.

"I'll wait here," I say, "with Martia." I'd rather stay with the housekeeper, whose services have come with the lease for as long as I can remember. For Martia, who's already abandoned us to prepare a welcome meal, everything centers on the kitchen. Mother and I aren't even allowed inside except to get a glass of iced tea or to sample sweets from a tray.

Mother's face goes flat, as if she's smoothing out emotion the way she would layer paint with a palette knife.

The scent of plantains mingles with burning motor oil from Jinco's taxi. As soon as Mother snaps the car door shut,

Jinco punches the horn—his usual way of announcing his arrival or departure—and floors the gas pedal. I lose sight of the car in the fine dust of the shell driveway. I imagine Mother sitting straight, her feet planted, staying balanced even as Jinco careens toward the airport. She is so practiced, so centered.

Martia appears in the doorway, wiping her hands on her apron. When I was little, I imagined the spices she mixed were like voodoo. I told Dad that if she wanted to, Martia could poison us. Dad laughed. Martia, though, said I was a smart girl, that you can't be putting the trust in just anyone. I trust Martia now.

"I'm okay," I say before she asks.

She shrugs, motioning me into the kitchen. From nowhere she hands me a plate of kokada.

"Kome," she says. "Eat." I start to say no, but I don't. I can't. I lift the first pink treat to my mouth, sucking in the sweet coconut taste.

Mother always refuses Martia's sweet offerings. She won't eat them.

I can't get enough.

Martia smiles and turns her back, leaving me the rest of the kokada. She starts to peel some just-cooked shrimp; their shells bubble like painful blisters in her hand. Her worn raffia scuffs sound like palm fronds as they brush the floor. She never seems to wear the new pairs Mother brings her every summer from Maine. Like mine, Martia's middle is wider this year, but she is comfortable with it. Her apron is stained with papaya and the essence of almond. She belongs to the house more than the absentee owner, who lives in Amsterdam and visits here in the winter months when the European skies turn gray.

Come to Curaçao, blue heaven. But Martia is not what the tourist brochures advertise with their slick, modern photographs: Perfect smiles. Thin bodies in thong suits lying underneath beach umbrellas, sipping cold drinks.

Except for the thong, that could be my mother on the cover of the brochures.

Cupping two more pieces of *kokada* in a napkin, I flee the safety of the kitchen. Martia's peeling mangoes now, letting the thin green skins plop into the sink. I hear her singing *tambú,* and I wonder what she thinks when she sings the old slave songs. I don't ask, though. Martia acts as if she doesn't know I've left the room, or where I might be going.

At the top of the metal staircase, I enter Mother's studio, the forbidden room. Martia cleans here only under Mother's direction, with any paintings in progress shielded from sight. Martia cannot risk looking and perhaps being fired.

From the studio windows, I notice the sea is the color of tumbled blue-green glass, roiled and unsettled. Last June after Dad died, his seat between Mother and me on the plane going home sat empty until just before takeoff, when a red-faced, sweating tourist weaved her way down the aisle and claimed it. She stuffed an oversized tote bag under the seat in front of her, leaving me to huddle against the window. As our plane rose into the sky, I couldn't take my eyes off the sea. I thought the color of the water might change with the light, but it didn't. It appeared deep blue, almost black, and dense as oil. No light penetrated the surface; we were left with the dark skin of the sea and no answers.

By now, the end of the first week of June at *Blauwe Huis*, Mother should be knee-deep in wet canvases, already ignoring me for the favorable slant of light under the eaves of the widow's walk. This spring she said the hot, dry island has been her "artistic touchstone" ever since she started coming here as a girl, and she had to come back, even this year, even after what happened. She insisted I come, too. We would start over.

Her canvases remain stretched and ready but empty, and her mixing palette has dried out, the smudges of blue paint wavy and stiff under my touch like a bad van Gogh imitation.

The tubes and glass bottles of paint feel cool in my hand. Mother's lined them up on the shelves like a display in a paint store, with the blues up front. She contemplates blue, collects it, honors it in every painting. Her marine blue appears steel gray, like a New England harbor in winter. Savannah blue acts sultry, with an undertone of indigo. Bahama blue seems paler than curaçao liqueur, more a bleached blue, the color of shallow water. It reminds me of the shade of Winslow Homer's Caribbean water, but not quite—as if for

Mother the sun has come on too strong, the glare blinding her to the undertones.

Mother chooses her blues carefully, with an eye toward the light, the swirl of colors on a glass palette tray. Fifteen years ago, she even named me for cyan, a fundamental blue.

On some mornings when she says she is working, I can stand down the beach, careful of the poisonous sap of the manchineel, and see her on the widow's walk, hand raised, holding a glass. Martia keeps the shelf in the dining room stocked with blue curaçao, the national liqueur, made from the bittersweet peel of the *apelsina*. Mother drinks it with bitter lemon soda over ice—a Blue Bay. Sometimes the light catches her drink glass like a prism. Maybe she is toasting the sea. If she is, she never acts drunk, not like my best friend Zoe's mother, who drinks when she thinks no one else is looking, but everyone knows.

Mother painted me blue, but as I look out over the sea, I think about Dad and wonder what color I really am.

What is the color for lost?

CHAPTER TWO

JINCO'S HORN BLARES outside. I blink, realizing I don't have any idea how long I've been standing here in Mother's studio. I brush my hand across the paints as if I'm touching an enemy and escaping unharmed. Palming a half-empty tube of Prussian blue paint, I slip it in my skirt pocket and run downstairs. Has any of the blue smudged onto my fingers, my clothes? I'm almost hoping it has, like a dare to my mother to notice.

Martia meets me in the kitchen. Her face doesn't give anything away. She knows where I've been, but she keeps it to herself. She opens the door and I step outside into the glare.

Looking like her photograph, Kammi exits the taxi's back seat from the left, close to me, Mother from the right. Trim and brunette and neat, Kammi's dressed out of Talbots down to the pink polo shirt and crisp capris. She's wearing sunglasses, so I can't see the color of her eyes, but I can tell there's not a trace of blue in her. She is pink, shell pink, like the inside of a conch shell before the sun has bleached it. Tender-skinned, she'll burn before the rest of us, turning the color of the cooked shrimp Martia peeled earlier.

The girl pulls a slim garment bag and a tote out of the cab. She has come with so little; I can't believe she's staying almost three weeks. Does she travel light because they teach that at her boarding school? Or is she simply like that, spare and contained? Though her bag is small, I imagine she's packed it tightly, properly, as if she's arranging small fish head to tail on top of each other. I shade my eyes with my hand, just to get a better view of her face around her sunglasses. Will she think Mother and I are allied against her for the rest of June at *Blauwe Huis*? She needn't worry. A gulf as wide as the Caribbean has come between my mother and me.

Kammi carries her own bags. She doesn't wait for Mother to help her, or even Jinco, who stirs himself only to carry Mother's luggage on the day we arrive and the day we leave.

The first time I remember coming to Curaçao—Mother, Dad, and me—I didn't understand where we were going or about beach living. I trailed beach sand into the rented house without thinking about it, Martia sweeping up behind me. I wanted to show Mother and Dad my sand castle, not realizing that it had slipped through my pudgy fingers with every step I took away from the water's edge.

Dad stopped coming a few years later, spending his summers in Europe on language tours, teaching American university students on their semesters abroad. He tried to explain, "Curaçao is your mother's place. There's no room for me there." I wanted to say there wasn't a place for me, either, but I didn't. Last year he finally came back, cutting short a tour through Italy to fly from Rome to Amsterdam to Curaçao. I traced the route on the map in the airline magazine I'd taken from our flight. Jinco deposited him at *Blauwe Huis* just before dusk and didn't carry his bags. Jinco's lack of interest in anyone's bags but Mother's bothered Dad, who was bleary-eyed from the flight. Mother told him to let it be. Jinco was reliable, she said, and had been so for years, and that was good enough for her. Dad grabbed his garment bag and left Mother to pay the fare.

Except for the luggage, Dad tried to make Mother happy those few weeks.

Kammi slips the garment bag over her bony left shoulder and walks toward me. As she does, a lizard skitters across the sand, trailing a shadow in front of her path. She doesn't miss a step. Maybe she didn't even see it. She extends her hand, almost as if she's auditioning to be queen.

"I'm so sorry . . ." she says as her cool hand touches mine in not quite a handshake, not an embrace. What is she sorry for? About my father? For the fact we'll be stepsisters?

I don't say anything. I turn away and lead her inside while Mother pays Jinco. Indoors, Kammi stops behind me for a moment, as if she's adjusting to the darker interior. I watch her as she takes off her sunglasses. Hazel, that's what color her eyes are.

"The shades were my mother's idea," she says, laughing in a timid way, her vowels soft and southern.

"This is yours." I point to the small room off the living area. "It was my mother's idea." I can't resist saying it that way. It really *was* Mother's idea to give Kammi my room, the nicer of the two small bedrooms. "Because," Mother said, "for now Kammi is a guest, not family. We want to make a good impression."

I put my things into the musty and unused second bedroom the day we arrived. The bedroom window faces the dry hills, not the water. I didn't even look at my old room. Martia, unaware of Mother's plan at first, had aired it out and tucked new hibiscus-colored sheets onto the bed. She told me she had found a pink paper fan shaped like a hibiscus blossom at a gift shop in Willemstad and she'd placed it on the pillowcase for me.

Perhaps it is destiny after all. The pink is perfect for Kammi. Dropping her bags on the bed, she smiles when she sees the fan and the sheets and the blue ocean beyond. *The sea, it is the sea.* Martia's voice in my head corrects me when I even think "ocean." To me, a sea sounds calm. An ocean doesn't.

Kammi pushes the curtains aside and stares at the water.

"That's the Caribbean," I tell her. "Curaçao's about forty miles from Venezuela." I sound like I've memorized the tourist brochures. By now I have.

"I thought people here would speak Spanish. I studied Spanish in school, but I don't like to speak it."

"Curaçao's a Dutch island. But some people speak Spanish. Papiamentu, the local language, is part Spanish and Portuguese, but other languages, too." Now I really sound like one of those tour guides who stand by the pier at St. Anna Bay and herd cruise-ship tourists on shopping trips that pretend to be cultural tours. Mother calls the tourists cattle. Another reason she says she won't display her artwork at the galleries in Willemstad.

"Do you speak it?" Kammi asks, turning to look at me.

"Papiamentu? No. I studied Arabic last year."

Her eyes go wide. I don't tell her I took the class to make Mother angry—she wanted me to study French. We were a class of five in an elective taught by a refugee. I got a C. I wouldn't turn in my homework.

I sense Mother listening from the hallway. Waiting to see how things go between us.

"Come on. I'll show you around." To my own ears, I sound polite. I hear myself as if I am standing outside my body, listening. "We're not on the Internet here. Except for the phone, we're in the Dark Ages." It doesn't bother me much, but I watch Kammi's face to see if she reacts. She simply nods. Her father must have warned her.

Mother's footsteps echo on the metal staircase as she goes up to her studio.

Kammi unfolds her bag onto the rattan luggage rack at

the foot of the bed. She unzips it, shakes out a few sundresses, all but unwrinkled, and hangs them in the closet. I was right: she packs like Mother, and her clothes are so tiny. I'd never fit in them. She leaves the rest and then follows me.

In the kitchen, Martia is smiling like she always does when she sees children.

"This is Martia," I say.

"*Bon bini*," Martia says. "Welcome." Martia wipes her hands on her apron and takes Kammi's small hands in hers, giving them a big squeeze. Not for the first time, I wonder what Martia's family is really like, what her children do while she's here with us. Martia only goes home on Sundays. Does she wonder, too, whether they think of her here in the fancy house?

"Thank you," Kammi says, smiling, a bigger smile than when she saw the pink-flowered bedroom.

"Such a pretty little girl come to Curaçao," Martia says. "You will be liking it here. You come see Martia you need anything. I make your favorite foods. So you no homesick." She shows Kammi the glass bowl. "Tonight we have shrimp and mango and a big salad. You like it?"

"Yes," Kammi says. I wonder if she is telling the truth or just being polite. The way she smiles, I bet she thinks Martia is unbiased, an ally.

She's wrong. Martia is mine.

CHAPTER THREE

COME ON, there's more to see," I say, motioning Kammi away from Martia, who is still smiling as she turns to continue preparing dinner.

Kammi follows me into the living room. Nature books and shells are arranged on the side tables. Big cushions with palm-tree prints line the white rattan furniture. Island décor just like something out of a magazine. Martia keeps everything looking that way. She sweeps the sand, fluffs the pillows, and repositions the shells.

"What's up there?" Kammi points to the metal staircase.

"You're not allowed up there." Like Bluebeard's castle.

Kammi's face goes sour.

"I'm not allowed up there, either," I say. "No one is. Except Mother. It's her studio." I picture the bottles and tubes of blue. Will Mother notice the Prussian blue is missing?

Maybe she'll assume the paint dried out in the bottom of the tube and she threw it away. Or maybe she'll think that she forgot she threw it away, because she drank too much. Yesterday, before she was even fully unpacked, I stole a nearly empty tube of Scarlet Lake from her art bin and dropped it in the garbage. If she missed it, she didn't say. It wasn't one of the blues, after all. The Prussian blue is still in my pocket. Evidence of a crime committed right under Mother's nose, but I can't bear to destroy it.

"Oh, I hope I get to see her work," Kammi says, and smiles. Her face lights up. "Before I came, she said I might. I want to paint, too."

The breath goes out of me. *Before she came.* All spring in Maine, Mother encouraged me to send Kammi a "get-acquainted e-mail." Kammi sent one to me, along with a photograph of herself under a beach umbrella. I couldn't make myself reply. I didn't have anything to say.

"Mother's very busy." That's a lie, but I say it anyway. "Come on. I'll show you the beach. There are places where you have to watch the riptide." I want out of the house.

I want *her* out of the house.

Before I open the French doors to the patio, the phone rings. Martia answers it in the kitchen. Her words turn stiff.

I hate it when the phone rings now. How the voice on the other end can change Martia with a simple hello. It's been that way since last year when the phone finally rang after Dad disappeared. Mother had been standing at the window facing the sea, as if she could will the boat to appear on the horizon. She didn't even turn when Martia answered the phone on the fourth ring, but I saw her face.

Martia walks into the living room. "It is Mayur Bindas. For you," she says, frowning. "I tell him you are busy. You have a guest." Martia is my ally, but Mayur and his parents are rich. They know the Dutch owner of this house. They might make things difficult for Martia if she were rude to Mayur.

"I'll take it." Mayur. I've been wondering when he'd call. He's waited until three days after we arrived. Mayur would wait just to make me wonder.

Kammi stands by the French doors, looking toward the sea, as if she's trying to give me some privacy. If she's curious about Mayur, she doesn't show it.

"Hello," I say into the phone.

"*Bon.*" Not "good afternoon" or "hello," just "good." Shorthand. I haven't heard Mayur's voice in a year. Not since the day before Mother and I left Curaçao. The day when we stopped at the Bindases' house to thank Dr. Bindas for his help with Dad on the beach. The day I pushed Mayur into the pool, still dressed in his best clothes from a family wedding he'd just attended, because of what he said to me.

"What do you want?" Last year, he said he had a secret I would want to know. He didn't get a chance to tell me and I didn't ask. So he has kept it for a whole year.

"Mamí said you were back. With a new girl." Without your father. He doesn't say it. But he pauses, so my mind fills the silence.

I don't say anything. Silence is a tactic I learned from the counselor Mother sent me to after we got back to Maine. Counselors like empty spaces. They know if they wait, the other person will fill up the space with words. Now I wait.

"Mamí told me you and the new girl must come to visit. You must come tomorrow," he says.

We haven't spoken in a year and he's already ordering me around. Or trying to.

"The new girl is Kammi." At her name Kammi turns around and cocks her head at me. She was listening after all.

"Kammi," he says. "Mamí says you and Kammi must come. Three in the afternoon. She says to bring your swimsuits."

"Your mother is very nice." Meaning he is not. "Tell her we'll come."

Kammi raises her eyebrows at me, asking me a question without speaking.

I shrug. After yelling to his mother that we're coming, Mayur starts to brag about some new game gadget he bought. How much it cost. I listen without hearing.

Then his voice gets low. "You remember what I said? Last year?"

Air rushes in my eardrum, as if the phone has become a shell and I can hear the sea.

"I'm hanging up," I say. I don't wait for Mayur to finish.

Mother's voice carries down the metal stairs. "Who was that?"

"Mayur."

"Bindas?"

"Yes." As if there were any other Mayur. "His mother invited Kammi and me over tomorrow at three."

Mother doesn't say "That's nice" or "I'm surprised after what happened." She just changes the subject. "Have you shown Kammi around?"

"We're going to the beach now." I shoo Kammi out the French doors. I'm closing them as I hear Mother start, "Be—"

Careful, she means to say.

I am past that point.

Outside, the sun is so bright it hurts my eyes. Kammi slips her sunglasses back on, but I just squint into the glare. I don't believe in sunglasses.

"Let's go," I say as we walk down the wooden steps of the deck and onto the sand. It squishes between my bare toes, so soft it almost tickles. Magic sand, Dad called it.

"Wait." Kammi pauses, tugging off her slides. Tiny, leather-soled, the shoes are a smaller version of Mother's. Like Mother, Kammi won't want them to get wet or covered in sand.

I feel Mother watching us, but I refuse to look up to the windows or the widow's walk beyond.

Instead, I dig my toes into the sand and wait. I brought

only two pairs of plastic flip-flops to wear, no nice shoes. For clothes, I packed two broomstick skirts, five T-shirts in pastel colors, enough underwear for a week, and a bathing suit with a ruffle at the bottom that Mother made me buy the week before we left. She said it would be flattering. She didn't say the ruffle would hide the roll of fat around my waist, the one I see her look away from whenever I lean over. Or that it would visually balance my growing breasts, which have expanded along with the rest of me this past year. She watched me slip the suit into my suitcase, on top. That's all I brought, though. Most of my summer clothes from last year don't fit anymore. Instead of telling Mother, I just stuffed towels in my suitcase to make it look full. I hate shopping, hate how nothing on the hangers looks right on me. As if the clothes belong to someone else and I'm just borrowing them.

Shoes off, Kammi nestles her pale toes in the sand. Even her toenails are pink.

Perfect. I laugh.

"What's so funny?"

I shake my head, glancing down at her feet and then at the water. "Nothing."

"What?" Frowning, she looks at her toes. "You don't like my nail polish?"

"No, I mean . . . sure, it's fine. Pink's perfect, really." For her. She's soft and easily burned.

But if I can see Kammi's pink, why can't I tell what color I am? Yesterday, I asked Martia what color she thought I was.

"Color?" she asked, as if she thought she'd heard me wrong.

"Yes, color. Like the way my name means 'blue,'" I said. "But what color do *you* think I am?"

She squinted at me, as if narrowing her vision until I appeared as just a color, no shape.

"Yellow," she said.

"Like sunshine?"

"Yellow like *kibrahacha*. Flowers, you know."

Actually, I didn't. Later I looked up the word in the guidebook to the flora and fauna of the Dutch Antilles. After the spring rains come, the western hills blaze up with yellow *kibrahacha*. Persistent, rangy, and rugged, they're all bloomed out by June when we arrive.

What did Martia mean? Am I really yellow?

At home in Maine, I have a book my father gave me about color. Goethe, a German philosopher, wrote it two hundred years ago. I keep it by my bed, moving the bookmark a page or two each night to keep Mother guessing about whether I'm reading it or not. Most of it bores me, and I skip pages, but I understand some of Goethe's ideas. He said color isn't just light hitting an object. Color is how we *perceive* light hitting an object. The color closest to light, he said, is yellow. The opposite, the color closest to the darkness—the absence of light—is blue.

I look past Kammi to the sea, but I don't say anything to her about the water or about color.

"Race you to the point." I burrow my feet into the sand, giving me traction and propelling me forward. I'm taller, longer-legged, and older than she is. I have the advantage.

I beat her, but she's not breathing as hard as me when she catches up. She turns to look back the way we came. Maybe she's trying to get her bearings, figuring out landmarks, making a map in her head.

"You can see the point for a long way down either beach. You won't get lost," I say.

"I just wanted to see what it looks like from here. The house."

I look, trying to imagine what it must be like to see it for the first time. From the beach side, you can see all three stories and the widow's walk on top. From the main entrance and driveway, which faces the hills, the house looks smaller—you can't see the ground floor. From here it looks like a castle, especially with the copper roof on the cupola, how it reflects the glare like a torch. I wonder if Dad saw it from the sea before the sun went down the first day he went missing.

"The Bindases live this way, around the point and along another cove. It's quicker to get there by going along the road."

"Who are the Bindases?" Kammi asks, still looking toward Blauwe Huis.

I know she's asking about Mayur. "Dr. Bindas is a doctor. Mrs. Bindas is very nice; pretty, too. You'll like her. They have a pool down by the sea."

"And Mayur?"

"You be the judge." I start to walk around the curve of the point, where I'll be out of sight of the house. "You'll meet him tomorrow. He's about fourteen." Older than Kammi, younger than me. All brat. What's he going to try to tell me?

"Who's waving? Is that your mother?" Kammi asks.

I turn around. Before I answer, Kammi starts waving back.

"Yes, it's her." I look down at the line of shells at the high-tide mark. I refuse to let Mother see me stare back at the house. Even when she is supposed to be painting, she is watching. I won't wave. It's not me she's waving to anyway. She's trying to impress Kammi, to make it seem as if we're a happy family. Or will be, once she marries Howard, Kammi's father.

Before Dad died, Mother's art students—her protégés, anyway—were the ones she tried to impress. Every year or two, she had a new favorite. They all had wonderful names, as if they'd been born to be artists: Catrione, Kiera, Samantha, Philippa.

Catrione was the one I liked best. She took time when Mother wasn't looking to show me things—how to arrange still-life objects to best effect, how to understand perspective. Things Mother lost patience in trying to explain to me. When Mother told me to think of an orchid in a vase as a cylinder, all I could see was the delicate lip of the blossom, the tiniest ruffles along the edges of the fragile petal, and the thin lines disappearing down its throat. I imagined the color turning darker and darker deeper inside the stem, and I wondered how that secret place could be painted. The next week, Mother bought a crochet hook and granny-square kit for me. "Some people are artists, some are craftsmen," she told me.

Catrione had more patience. Once, she even sneaked to my room while Mother was out talking to a gallery owner. She looked over my sketch of the orchid, which I kept under the cloth runner on my dresser. Hidden, but close to the surface.

Philippa was Mother's last student. She was around the longest and was the most like Mother. She trashed more canvases than all the other students combined. I'd find a canvas by the curb on garbage day, and I couldn't see why it had been tossed away. Even Dad, who didn't "involve himself" with Mother's art, rescued a couple of Philippa's paintings and hung them where the light showed them off.

"She's a perfectionist," Mother explained as she straightened one of Philippa's rescued paintings. She said it as if that was a good thing. I thought of the tangled skein of yarn in the back of my closet.

I am tracing the outline of a broken whelk with my finger when Kammi's shadow falls over me and blocks the light. I hold the shell up for her to see. The inside is still shiny lavender.

"Do you go shelling?" she asks, picking up an open coquina, still connected at the center so it looks like wings.

"I go out early." Not to collect shells but to scavenge for

sea glass. "It's best in the morning, just after high tide. Before anyone else gets there." I hate it when I find fresh footprints there before me. I always wonder what treasure others have stolen.

"These are all over Florida. We stay at Sanibel Island every summer. Mom once made a soup out of coquinas I gathered. I wouldn't eat it."

I reach down and scoop up a still-whole scallop shell. I hold it out to Kammi, who takes it in both hands.

Kammi's parents are both still alive. Every time Mother tried to tell me about Howard saying "Kammi did this" or how "Howard and Kammi did that," I wouldn't listen. I didn't want to hear about her or her father, especially not about them together.

"Come on." I want away from the sight of the house. I start running.

"Wait up!" Kammi's voice is broken by the wind in my ears.

CHAPTER FOUR

I JOG ALMOST all the way to the beginning of the Bindases' property, but I stop before crossing over onto it. I don't want Mayur to see me. He might think I've come to talk to him, that I'm eager to hear his secret. Last year, when he claimed he knew something about what happened, I thought he was lying. What could he know? When he tracked me down by e-mail, I blocked his messages. Back here on the island, I still think he's lying, but I need to know what he thinks he knows.

Walking back toward *Blauwe Huis*, I meet Kammi, who apparently followed me. She isn't running, just walking, as if she knew she'd find me.

"Where'd you go?" she asks.

I shrug.

She waits a moment for me to answer. When I don't,

she asks, "Is that a canal?" She points to a dry ravine coming from the hillside all the way to the shore.

"When it rains hard—not all that often—the water runs off down the hills and out to sea. Once, we found a dead goat on the beach there." Last year, Dad and I took a walk every morning down to this area where, if there wasn't any haze, we could see another island.

"Yuck," she says.

I ask, "Do you swim?"

She beams. "Sure. I took lessons. Last year I swam at the country club where we belong. What about you?"

"I know how." I don't swim, though. Not anymore. "Watch for undertow here."

Kammi's smile fades.

My lips turn up. "We better go back. Martia's making a special dinner. For you."

For Martia's sake, I don't want to be late.

We walk in silence, listening to the surf. Kammi's steps start to match mine, even though my stride is longer. I wonder if it really is true, that women who live together start to have periods at the same time, and they aren't even aware of it happening. Does Kammi have periods? Is she too young? Mother and I don't discuss periods anymore. I buy extra supplies so I don't run out and have to ask her.

"Hey, look." Kammi points to a wooden building tucked into the manchineel. "Is there a sailboat? Can we take it out?"

She doesn't wait for an answer. She runs to the boathouse and pulls on the door. Padlocked. I could have told her that. She stands on tiptoe and peers through a cloudy window, cupping her hands around her eyes so she can see inside.

"We don't have a sailboat." I know what she'll see, even though I haven't looked myself this summer. Fishnets nailed to the wall, as if they're still drying after a long day in the water. A fishing boat, yes, but the motor's gone, and the blue paint's chipping off.

Mother painted *The Nautilus* two summers ago as a favor to the Dutch owner. He'd named the boat after the submarine in Jules Verne's *20,000 Leagues Under the Sea*, his favorite book. Dad took the boat out twice last summer to fish in deep water when he heard the fish were running.

Once, he came back with fish.

The second time, he did not come back.

Unlike the blue boat, a real nautilus shell has dozens of chambers filled with air. The animal inside lets out air to maneuver itself into the depths of the sea, taking oxygen with it to the bottom. Is there enough air for a person to breathe? If you could cup the shell to your mouth under water and inhale, could you get enough air to get to the surface if you were drowning?

"Come on, we'll be late," I tell Kammi, picking up my pace. Not looking at the boathouse. It's not that I care about being late, it's more that I don't want Martia to think I don't love her.

Mother's waiting for us at the French doors. Did she notice Kammi at the boathouse?

"Nice to see you two getting acquainted," Mother says. She sweeps her arm out, motioning us toward the house like a stage director. "Miss Kammi, please lead us in to dinner." She acts as if we're at a royal court in some play. Martia will serve us golden trays of figs, pomegranates, and other delicacies while we lean back against soft floor pillows.

For this we need an entrance. "Bring on the trumpets," I say.

"What?" Mother asks.

"Crumpets. I wonder. Shall we have crumpets with our tea?" I imitate the British accent of Philippa. She'd been studying in Italy last year, but she was in Maine when we got home. And she was the only one of Mother's art students to attend the memorial service. Mother didn't talk to her. Philippa sat a row behind Mother and me, and I heard her tell someone she couldn't believe how the sky could be so blue, so clear and cloudless, on such a sad day.

Kammi giggles. She's probably thinking that we're joking, like all families do. I curtsey, the damp edges of my skirt sweeping the wooden planks as I trail Kammi inside, leaving Mother to follow us both.

Kammi folds her sunglasses and tucks them beside her plate, just so. She bows her head for a moment. I can't believe she's praying.

When she opens her eyes, I say, "Are you okay?"

Mother laughs. "Don't be ridiculous, Cy. Kammi's fine."

Kammi blushes, and I pass her the shrimp platter.

Except for my friend Zoe, I don't know anyone who says grace. Suddenly, I want to ask Kammi about God and how she knows God exists. Is God more than a feeling inside? Does she believe because her parents told her to, or does she believe because nothing else makes sense? When even a simple flower is so perfect, it can't have been due to chance.

Maybe I will pray, too, at our next meal, if only because Mother won't be able to say anything. But whatever Mother thinks about God or church, she wouldn't question Kammi. So how could she question me? Not like when Mother wouldn't let me attend Zoe's church, not even after Dad died.

"What church do you go to?" I ask. Maybe it's something exotic—a group of snake-handling fanatics. But it can't be. Not for a girl who attends boarding school in Atlanta.

"Episcopal."

Of course. A church for rich people.

"Don't they have priests?" I ask.

Kammi tilts her head to one side, as if she's thinking about my question.

"Yes," she says. "But they're not like Catholic priests. They can marry."

She blushes, and I bet it's because she was talking about marriage and thinking about sex, and those are subjects we're not ready to talk about. Not even Mother, who uses the tongs to serve herself salad. She passes the bowl to Kammi, who arranges salad on her plate as if it's an art display. Maximizing texture and color, minimizing blank space. They both do it, seemingly without thinking. With a pang, I realize Kammi is an artist.

"Is your dad Episcopal, too?" Howard hasn't mentioned religion in the times we've been together, but with me he's stiff and formal. He stands in doorways, as if he isn't sure whether to enter or retreat. Whether he can calculate the business of stepdaughters the way he does a profit margin. Suddenly, I want to know what his beliefs are. What if he believes in purgatory or converts dead people from his family tree?

Mother and Kammi both say no at the same time.

Kammi pierces her salad with her fork. "He says he can't prove God exists." She speaks as if she's not sure he's right, but she's still young enough to believe fathers are infallible and will live forever.

Martia hovers by the dining table. She pats Kammi's thin wrist. "Kome, kome," she says. "Eat, eat." After she circles us, and sees that our plates are full, she retreats. I hear the soft crackle of the radio turning on in the kitchen.

"The Bindases have invited you over for a swim tomorrow." Mother addresses Kammi. "They have a son"—she squints at Kammi—"about your age, I think."

"I told her all about Mayur," I say. I didn't, of course. Only his name and age. But Mother doesn't know what I said or didn't say.

"I'm sure Kammi will give Mayur a chance." Mother

turns to her. "He's a nice-enough boy. From a privileged immigrant family. So his expectations are high."

"She means he's slumming," I say.

Mother glares at me. "He's lonely."

"With all those cousins who come from Trinidad?"

"But they don't live here."

"Neither do we."

"His parents like him to meet new people. It was very nice for him to call this year. Particularly when you were so rude." Mother leaves out why I was rude. "I'm sure he'll like Kammi." Because Kammi is nice and I am not, that's what she means.

I don't bother to warn Kammi that Mayur is a smirky rich kid who set the rules for the pool when his parents aren't around. The first time I was invited over, he said that I had to take a shower—with soap—or I couldn't swim in his pool. His pool, he called it. The houseboy delivered fresh towels folded in squares, just like at a hotel. They smelled like lemons and bleach.

"The pool's nice," I concede to Kammi. "The way it seems to be part of the sea, but isn't. It's safer."

I won't let Mother have the last word.

CHAPTER FIVE

A FEW MINUTES before three the next after-
noon, I tap on Kammi's door. It snaps open as if she's been
waiting just on the other side since lunch. Dressed for a pool
party, she's braided her brown hair and pinned it up at the
back. A pareo is tied just so at her right hip, where the
barest pink bikini bottom peeks through; the bikini top is
held by what looks like ribbons over her shoulders. Somehow she managed to pack in her suitcase a straw tote with a
pink gingham lining that matches her suit. Her whole look is
so fragile, I have to turn away.

I say, "Hope you brought enough sunscreen." I sound like
my mother. When she addresses me it's not in direct questions
like "Did you bring concealer?" or orders like "Don't eat that."
Instead, she says "Ice cream has X grams of fat" when I'm not
even close to the refrigerator, or "Black is slimming" when I'm

reading a book in the bay window on a winter night in Maine. Funny, she doesn't say that about my black beaded headscarf, the one I started wearing after Dad died and I signed up for Arabic. Mother hates that scarf. But I liked wearing it sometimes last year, covering myself like my Arabic teacher. After a while, the principal said no one could cover their hair at school unless they had a written note from a parent saying their religion required such a covering. Even then, he wasn't happy about it. He was afraid someone would smuggle a weapon into the school under a scarf. As if it wouldn't be easy enough to do that anyway if someone wanted to.

Outside, I feel my bathing suit sticking to my skin underneath the same skirt and T-shirt I've been wearing all day. If I go in the pool, I'll take the skirt off and leave on the tee. It skims the top of my thighs and helps cover my chest better than the swimsuit. As long as I don't get wet, the tee hides the fat.

Will Mayur notice I've gotten fat? Heavier up top like the boys in my class started to notice this year, and I hated the way they made fun. Zoe told me to ignore them, but it was easier for her. She's petite like Kammi.

We're away from the house before Kammi says anything.

"Do you really dislike . . ." Kammi starts to ask. I think she's going to ask me why I don't like my mother. "Why don't you like Mayur?"

She doesn't ask about Mother. That's a subject she's probably not ready to talk about.

"He's a jerk," I say. "But his parents are nice. The pool, too, like I said." It's also away from my mother. And even if I don't like him, I have a reason to see Mayur again.

At the next turn in the road, I lead us along a shell path that winds down a hill toward a secluded bay shaped like a thin lip of moon. When we reach a steep turn, Kammi's leather-bottomed shoes slip.

She skids, catching herself before she lands on her butt.

"Flip-flops or sneakers. Don't you have some?" I look at her and then turn away. I'm more direct than Mother after all.

"Running shoes, I have those," she says, pushing herself up.

I start walking. "Next time, wear them. Something with grip."

She doesn't answer, but she starts to place her feet more carefully as we walk. She won't slip again.

The path widens to a shell driveway, and suddenly a lawn spreads out in front of us. It is lined by rocks and irrigated green. The Bindases aren't into native flora, like the Dutch owner of our house. He asks the gardener to plant only indigenous plants, the hearty ones that don't need extra watering from the cistern. Martia says he is "respectful" of Curaçao. Whenever Mother mentions the lovely calla lilies in the Bindases' yard, Martia doesn't say anything about the neighbors. She hides her opinions behind her apron.

In the Bindases' yard, the gardeners are working, digging up piping, moving whole rows of lilies still in bloom. The blossoms have wilted, collapsed into the texture of wet paper. Only the birds of paradise remain stubbornly upright.

Mrs. Bindas waves from the deck along the pool. She's dressed in flowing yellow palazzo pants—an unsuccessful attempt by overweight women to hide their thighs, my mother would say. I say Mrs. Bindas isn't heavy. The billowy pants make her look even thinner, slender and light as a swallowtail butterfly. She calls into the shadows of the house. "Mayur, come, please. Your guests are here."

By the time Kammi and I reach the deck, Mayur is stalking out of the house.

I introduce Kammi to Mrs. Bindas. Kammi shakes her hand like a grown-up.

"I'm very glad you're staying next door this month. So nice for Cyan and her mother to have some company." She pauses, maybe thinking how Kammi might help us forget last year. Of course, she doesn't say any more about that. "And for Mayur, too. He craves having other children of his—you know—age. Before his cousins come, he gets—how do you say? Bored?"

When Mayur saunters forward, Kammi even holds out her hand to him, but he just says hi to her over his shoulder and heads to the pool. He doesn't even look at me. Short, with dark eyes that might look cute on anyone else, he snaps on goggles and flings himself into the pool, splashing water our way.

Mrs. Bindas titters like a bananaquit. "Oh, Mayur, he is

showing off. Just a little for his guests." She looks at Mayur's back as he paddles across the pool, and I see a frown furrow her brow. "I'll send out some refreshments."

I give Kammi a look. Mayur showing off—as if that's something new.

Kammi shrugs and scoots a lounge chair into the shade. She slips her sunglasses on, steps out of her shoes, and settles them under the chair, toes pointing away from the pool, heels touching. So perfectly placed. Balanced. Just the way Mother would do it. For a second, I wonder if Kammi is really the daughter and I am the stepdaughter-to-be. Is that what Mother wants?

I toss my flip-flops. One lands upside down in the puddle created by Mayur's dive.

Kammi retrieves a horse club mystery from her beach bag.

"Aren't you too old for those?" I ask.

She looks a little embarrassed. "My grandmother sent them to me for the trip. I have to tell her I've read them. I don't want to hurt her feelings."

I laugh. "Why don't you just memorize the blurb on the back, in case she asks?"

"They're not that bad."

"If you don't mind the dumb dialogue and the stupid endings, and how everyone always learns something about themselves. I hate books like that." Because life isn't like that. Sometimes, people disappear and there aren't any lessons to be learned. Only questions left unanswered.

"I just can't lie," she says. She acts as if I've asked her to lie about something important.

"Suit yourself." Closing my eyes, I settle back in the lounge chair, ignoring Mayur as he does the butterfly down the length of the pool. Leave it to him to choose the splashiest swim stroke. The one that says "Look at me."

A few minutes later, water droplets land on my ankles.

"Stop that, Mayur." I know it's him before I open my eyes.

"It's my pool," he says, splashing from the middle of the pool.

"They're my legs."

"My chair."

"They're still my legs." I can't believe I'm saying this.

Beside me, Kammi dog-ears the page she's reading. She closes the paperback and tosses it on top of her beach bag.

She actually asks Mayur a question. "Are you on a swim team?"

He stops splashing. He can't help himself. Someone's interested in him. He swims to the edge of the pool and plants his head on his folded arms while the rest of him floats in the water. His mouth reaches just out of the water. His goggles add to the idea that he could be a space alien or something.

"The school doesn't have one. I'm on a club team, though."

I drape my arm across my forehead. *A club team.* I'm surprised he didn't say it was *his* team.

"I'm joining our club team next year, too," she tells him.

Kammi can play his game, but she's nice when she does it. I grin to myself.

"How big's your school?" he asks.

"Two hundred students. How about yours?"

Mayur pushes himself back into the water, lets his head go under. Obviously his school has fewer than two hundred students.

I laugh out loud this time. I don't think Mayur hears a thing, with his ears full of water. But Kammi does. She smiles, seeming to know she's bested Mayur at his own game. Whether the smile is supposed to include me, I don't know.

Mayur retreats to the farthest corner of the pool.

Kammi takes her sunglasses off and places them on the wrought-iron table. She unknots the pareo and slides into the water in one smooth motion.

Using a graceful breaststroke, Kammi swims the length of the pool and back. Her moves make barely any splash. I watch Mayur watching her. I can't tell what he's thinking.

Almost without slowing down, Kammi slips out of the water like a seal. As she's drying off, Mrs. Bindas returns to the pool area.

Behind her, the houseboy is carrying a platter with a huge bowl piled high with something frozen, yellow and white with slivers of shaved coconut scattered on top. He nearly trips when he sees Kammi stretched out on the deck chair, damp, like a model spritzed with water on the cover of a fitness magazine, her hair still braided. She doesn't even notice. She's sitting up, adjusting the pareo, then her shoulder strap, barely breathing hard from the swim.

"Gelato," Mrs. Bindas says. "Piña colada flavor. No alcohol, of course." She titters again, in that high-pitched way, as if she is making another joke, and waves us over to the large wrought-iron glass-topped table in the shade.

The houseboy spoons gelato into bowls and passes the first to Kammi, of course. Her pink skin glows just the way the makeup ads promise.

"Mine—" Mayur starts to say as the houseboy finishes filling a second bowl, but his mother interrupts him.

"Guests always go first," Mrs. Bindas says.

Mayur pouts, but he's smart enough not to say anything that will embarrass him in front of his company. Even if he doesn't treat us special unless his mother is around.

I am given the second bowl, though the houseboy barely glances at me as he slides it across the glass table in my direction. Last year, I was the only guest, served first. The houseboy scoops out a double amount for Mayur, who snatches it away almost before the serving spoon clears the edge of the bowl. He plops himself into the chair farthest from the table and slurps his ice cream. Either Mrs. Bindas doesn't hear him or she doesn't care.

"It's delicious. Thank you." Kammi is polite, so predictable. I wonder if she ever surprises herself.

"Thank you." I don't trust myself to say more. Mrs. Bindas hasn't yet referred to last summer.

Mrs. Bindas folds her hands together as if she might clap. She's pleased with her gift. And with the response from the American girls.

"The flowers are so beautiful here. What are those?" Kammi says, pointing to an area on the other side of the pool, undisturbed by the gardeners.

"Birds of paradise, you call them in English. Mrs. Walters, she told me that one year. She sat here in this very garden and drew so many of our plants. That's bougainvillea over the wall."

Mrs. Bindas is gracious when talking about my mother. If she remembers the last time I was here, a year ago, when Mayur landed in the pool in his dress shoes and suit, she doesn't act like it. Mother made me come with her to thank Dr. Bindas in person for his assistance. The Bindases had just come from a family wedding. "My cousin, he knew about your father," Mayur said to me. "What happened with the boat." I heard the sea in my ears, felt waves crashing over me. I couldn't breathe.

Mayur told me his cousin knew something about what happened with the boat. "How calm the sea was that day, how flat," he said. The police found a bottle of champagne, unopened, set in water in an ice bucket. When the police lifted the bottle from the bucket, the wrinkled label peeled off. Almost like skin off a bone. Mayur said there was more, a mystery. "Who takes champagne on a boat alone?" he asked. "Maybe there were two dead bodies from the boat. Maybe there's still a dead body out there. I know something, too." That's when I pushed Mayur, and he flailed backwards into the pool.

Mayur should have whined to his mother that I was to blame, but he didn't. He told her he tripped into the pool and she sent him to change his clothes. Mrs. Bindas followed close behind him like a sheepdog, reminding him he should be careful. "You could have hit your head. And your suit, Mayur. It is ruined."

I retreated to the door, where Mother was speaking to Dr. Bindas. He handed her a book he said had been Dad's, something he'd left by the pool one day. Mother took the book without looking at it.

That was the last visit. Mother and I left Curaçao the next day, stuffing clothes and unread books into suitcases and a few of Mother's most precious paints into her carry-on bag instead of toothpaste and cosmetics. She left the water-splotched book Dr. Bindas had given her on the coffee table when she took her luggage to the door, where Jinco waited with the taxi. Dad's *The History of Language*. I slipped it into my suitcase without saying anything to Mother about it. We rode to the airport in a silence we have clung to ever since.

Mrs. Bindas is talking, describing the landscaping, how many gardeners had to be hired to make it work. Mayur is still eating, and is tapping his bare foot against the chair leg. Mrs. Bindas turns to me.

"The garden is so perfect this year. I am hoping Mrs. Walters will come here and teach an afternoon workshop. I have a few friends who like to paint."

The gelato gives me a chill. Mother never likes to teach groups of women, the ones who are middle-aged, too rich, with no talent. Those with money enough to buy the best supplies and the best instructors.

Kammi looks at me to answer, but when I don't speak, she says: "Oh, I'm sure she would be happy to have a class. Though she's so busy, you know. An artist must concentrate on her own work first."

Kammi sounds like a recording. I hear Mother's inflection when Kammi says "concentrate on her own work." Mother takes on students here and there—but only those who are young, talented, and hungry, very hungry to learn. Catrione quit three winters ago, a month or two after Mother scolded her for spending an afternoon a week after high school art class to tutor other students who were behind. For giving me hints when she thought Mother wasn't listening. I overheard Mother lecturing Catrione in the studio, where I was no longer welcome. Because I did not follow her directions. Because I was not serious.

Someone touches my arm. It's Kammi. She frowns at me. "I'm sure she would. Right, Cyan?"

I look at Mrs. Bindas's expectant face. Maybe she's

thinking that this is the least Mother could do. After the incident at the pool, after Dr. Bindas went down to the beach that night to identify my father. And though the Bindases have been our neighbors here for years, Mrs. Bindas has never asked for anything from my mother.

"I don't know. I'll mention it to her." Even though I know she won't want to do it.

Inside, a chime rings. Mrs. Bindas flits away, calling over her shoulder about the phone, winking at Mayur and reminding him to ask us about next week.

The houseboy follows Mrs. Bindas, though he turns briefly to look again at Kammi just before he enters the shadow of the house. Mayur waits until the houseboy disappears before he scoots over and scoops out more gelato for himself. A scoop for Kammi, too. Then the gelato is gone, a melted yellow pool in the bottom of the dish, a sprinkling of stray coconut.

Mayur clinks his spoon against his teeth as he rushes to finish the gelato in his bowl before his mother returns.

"Next week we're having bonfires on the beach." He stretches his arms out wide. "With a big cookout. Another family, the Garças, will come, too. And my cousins will be here. You're all invited." He looks at Kammi. He's ignoring me on purpose. "Mother hires a girl to write the envelopes, a calligrapher," he says. "She uses real gold dust in her inks." He says this to impress Kammi.

Kammi oohs and aahs in the right places.

Mayur finally looks at me. "And bonfires," he says to me. "Huge bonfires up and down the beach. To toast marshmallows. You do that in America, right?"

Memories of bonfires make me shiver.

Kammi answers for me. "Yes, marshmallows and bonfires. Our town does a picnic once a summer."

"But on the beach. Late into the night?" Mayur is taunting me, and Kammi has no clue. She doesn't know what happened last year. Mother hasn't told her. Neither has Howard.

I clink the spoon into my bowl. I squint at the lowering sun.

"It's time to go."

Kammi looks sideways at me, but she doesn't argue. I'm in charge.

Like Mayur, I take pleasure in small victories.

CHAPTER SIX

MOTHER'S WAITING for Kammi and me in the living room when we slip through the door.

"Come on out here." She waves us through the open French doors and onto the deck.

Kammi obeys immediately, not even stopping by her room to drop off her straw tote. Maybe she thinks she'll get Mother's attention now, and that she'll have the chance to talk about painting.

I follow, a few beats behind. It might be worth it to hear the conversation. I wonder how Mother will frame the words, how she'll make everything she says sound like she has only Kammi's interests in mind.

Mother has arranged herself on the lounge chair facing the sea. A still-life composition. This late in the afternoon, the sun is behind the house, and we're in the shadows, where it isn't too hot.

"Sit, sit. I want to hear all about it," Mother says, too cheerful.

In the kitchen, Martia bangs the pans and dishes she's clearing away. Her rhythm sounds off. Did Mother find food hidden in my room? Did she scold Martia for it? How many times has she told Martia that coconut is not good for me? The kokada she makes is too fattening.

Even though the kitchen doesn't sound like it's supposed to, the smells of fish with lemon and funchi—fried corn-bread—tease me. Despite the gelato I've eaten, my stomach whines.

Kammi sits in the chair closest to Mother. "Mrs. Bindas is really nice." She doesn't bring up right away that Mrs. Bindas wants Mother to hold an art workshop for her and her friends. Maybe she senses that Mother won't be thrilled. Or maybe she wants Mother all for herself. "She told us about her gar-den." Kammi describes the birds of paradise and the vines that cascade over the low stone wall. Mother nods as Kammi talks. I close my eyes and I can see everything just as she says.

Mother sips a Blue Bay drink while she listens to Kammi. Curaçao tastes so sweet it makes my throat ache. Last summer Dad and I toured the distillery. The tour guide said that the Spaniards brought the original orange trees from Valencia. In the dry soil of Curaçao, though, the oranges produced only tart fruit. People later found a way to turn the bitter fruit into something sweet. At the end of the tour, Dad bought a crate of liqueur in all its colors—blue, red, green, and mandarin. Last year he poured me a thimble-sized drink for toasting when we celebrated Mother's upcoming one-woman show, what she called a retrospective, at a gallery in Atlanta. The retrospective wasn't opening until October. After Dad died, the gallery asked Mother if she wanted to cancel. Mother said no, the art could be a tribute. Except that the art was never about Dad.

I sit on the rattan hassock. Taking my feet out of my flip-flops, I cross my legs under my skirt.

"What did you think of the Bindases' house?" Mother asks Kammi, and then answers her own question in the same breath. "It's grand, isn't it."

Kammi freezes for a second. "We didn't go inside. But if the inside is like the pool and patio, it must be beautiful, too," she says a moment later. "Mrs. Bindas served us gelato."

Mother's gaze flickers my way. "I hope it doesn't spoil your appetites. Martia's grilled red snapper."

I stare straight back at her.

Kammi says quickly, "Mayur says they're having a cookout on the beach next week."

Mother smiles. "The Bindases' house is on the prettiest stretch of beach on this part of the island. The view is unsurpassed." She means the view from the Bindases' house is better than the view from here.

"Did you swim?" Mother asks me.

"No," I say. "Mayur took up the whole pool with his butterfly stroke."

Mother raises her eyebrows.

"I barely got wet," Kammi says, as if she's apologizing to Mother for my not having gone in. She doesn't make a big deal of her own lap.

"Mayur is exuberant." Mother raises the back of the lounge chair so she sits straighter.

"He does seem to like the pool," I say, thinking back on last summer.

Mother frowns and starts to say something, but Martia appears at the French doors, and the moment passes. She's holding an envelope in front of her, away from her body, as if it contains bad news.

She reaches out to Mother. "The postman just came. I signed for a letter."

Signing for a letter is not always good, not even here, where every aspect of life is more formal than at home. After Dad died, Mother complained about all the letters she had to sign for. How she had to get dozens of copies of the death certificate. I still have a copy in my room, hidden inside *The History of Language*. The original document was written in Dutch, with a certified English translation attached. I read and reread the English version so many times I memorized it.

It said so little to be so important.

Mother takes the envelope. "They let you sign for it?"

"*Sí*," Martia says. Martia is local, trusted. I'm sure the postman knows her better than anyone else who stays in *Blauwe Huis*, probably even better than the owner.

A smaller envelope is tucked inside the larger one, like a wedding invitation. It is stamped with a seal, protecting the contents, like one of the medieval parchments written in old Italian that Dad would sometimes translate for a history scholar.

Mother's fingers slide under the flap and break the seal. She opens it, peeks in, almost as if she's seeing if it will bite. She tugs out a page.

"What is it?" I ask.

"I can't read it." Mother turns the paper over, as if she expects a translation on the back. "It's all in Dutch."

"Martia can translate," I say.

Martia shrugs. "*Sí*."

Mother doesn't hand the paper over. Instead, she beckons Martia to come read over her shoulder.

Martia mouths the words silently before she starts speaking. "It is from the lawyer here. Just closing out the files, passing along a copy of the commissioner's final report on Mr. Walters's death, that the incident was wholly accidental."

Mother shifts in her chair. "Well, this is ridiculous. They concluded all of this last year. Why would the lawyer send out another letter?"

Kammi looks at me. Maybe she thinks I can answer the riddle.

Martia says, "This is what the lawyer says, just closing the file. Formal." She shrugs, as if to apologize for the bureaucracy that sends a letter a year after the fact.

"Why does he have to stir things up again?" Mother takes another swig of her blue drink. "I paid his fees."

"He's not even right," I say.

"What?" Mother asks.

"It wasn't wholly an accident. Was it?"

Mother blanches. She let down her guard and asked a question she didn't want the answer to. "Cyan, please stop. We've been over this before."

Yes, we've been over it before. Mother says what happened was an accident. The articles published in the local paper after it happened said it was an "incident." An incident is not the same as an accident. An accident is a mistake. I don't know if what happened was a mistake. No matter what the commissioner's report says.

Martia steps between Mother and me. "Miss Kammi, please come in, we will have dinner now. You, too, Cyan." Martia touches Kammi on the shoulder and Kammi follows.

"I'm not really hungry," she says. She slides her straw bag onto her arm and slips into the house. "The gelato . . ."

Martia follows her like a mother hen. I don't move.

Mother snaps her head in my direction. "What are you doing? Are you trying to make things hard? After everything that's happened, why can't you just be nice?" Mother keeps talking, not waiting for—not wanting—an answer from me.

"You know all about it, do you?" Mother's voice turns as icy as the drink she's guzzling. "We'll talk about this later." With trembling hands she struggles to force the paper back into the envelope. After a moment, she closes it as if it contains some evil spell.

Mother stalks inside and up the stairs to her studio. Even from out here, I can hear her footsteps clang on the metal staircase.

Martia flutters between the kitchen and the dining table, where I go to sit, alone. Dinner is ruined. The fish, cooked too long, has turned to rubber. The fried cornbread congeals in my mouth. It doesn't want to go down, but I swallow it anyway, piece after piece, until it's all gone. Every crumb.

CHAPTER SEVEN

JUST AFTER DAWN the next morning, when I slip
in from the beach, my pockets weighted down with shells
and sea glass, I hear Mother's footsteps going up the metal
staircase. I catch her glance as she's closing the door to her
studio. I can't tell what she's thinking and I don't care. The
damp hem of my skirt drags on the floor and my flip-flops
squish as I walk through the kitchen, leaving a trail of sand.
Martia doesn't scold, though. She lets me squeeze past her
and into Mother's still-warm chair. Without speaking, she
hands me a plate of pancakes topped with coconut syrup. My
favorite breakfast.

Mother paces upstairs. No matter how softly she walks,
I always know when she's up there. If she's aware of my ven-
tures into her studio, she hasn't let on. She hasn't mentioned
the missing tubes of oil paint. Maybe she hasn't noticed yet.

Kammi tiptoes into the kitchen in her bare feet, her pink toenails like small shells, ever so quiet on the woven rug. She must not realize Mother is already awake and she's afraid to disturb her.

Martia turns and smiles at Kammi. *"Bon bini,"* she says. Good morning, as if yesterday afternoon were only a bad memory. She wipes her floury hands on her apron and reaches out to guide Kammi to a chair, then places a glass of pink guava juice in front of her.

"You missed the pancakes with coconut syrup," I say, licking the last of the syrup off my fork. I feel overfull. Maybe the rich coconut will make me sick. But in an hour or two, I'll be hungry again. Martia will sneak food into my room later.

Mother hasn't looked in my room here on the island. Back home in Maine this past year, she searched my dresser drawers, trying to root out the candy wrappers and the chip bags as if they were weeds in a garden. Leaving ads for one-hundred-calorie snacks pinned to the corkboard on my bedroom door. That and notes on the kitchen counter. *Working late. Lean De-Lite entrée in freezer.* That's how we communicated most of the time.

Since we arrived here this year, she uses Martia to give me messages instead of leaving notes. She gets Martia to say "The colas are no good for you." Yet Martia still ladles extra servings for me at meals and bakes coconut candies for dessert.

Kammi shrugs, not making a fuss about the pancakes. But I see in her eyes just a hint of disappointment.

"Oh, *chookie*, don't you worry. I make you something good," Martia says. Martia called me *chookie*, too, when I was younger. In Papiamentu, it means "chick." I feel as if I have always been Martia's chick, taking shelter under her arms when she clucks.

"So what are you going to do today?" Martia asks me while she's whipping up something light and fluffy. The thin batter spreads across the heated pan like foam from a wave. Finer than pancakes, crepes are Kammi's reward. "You show Miss Kammi around, yes?"

I shrug. No, that's what I want to say. I want to sit on the beach and stare at the sea and do nothing. Martia's so eager, though, that for once I can't say what I want.

Kammi answers for me. "I want to paint." She smiles. I bet she's pleased with herself for speaking up, especially after yesterday. "I have to practice. Dad expects me to learn something while I'm here. I started a scene in my head last night. The boathouse."

The sweet taste on my tongue goes sour.

Martia doesn't miss a beat. "I'm sure Mrs. Walters will be happy to show you some hints, but today is not so good. Mrs. Walters, she is very busy. She has a big commission to finish."

Martia is capable of lying. For the first time, I know for certain she's told a lie. Mother has no commission. She isn't busy. As of yesterday, the canvases stood empty. Some pencil lines suggested Mother might be starting something, but it's hard to tell.

Kammi's face falls. She hasn't learned yet to hide the things that matter most.

"I have just the good idea, what you should do," Martia said, serving Kammi her crepes. "I make you a picnic lunch, and you can take it to Boca Roja Beach. Miss Cyan, she knows the way." Martia bustles around the kitchen. She lines a cooler with blue plastic ice packs, the ones Mother brought from home years ago, handling them as if they possess magic. She packs waxed-paper packets of food inside, along with a bottle of water and two lemon-lime sodas.

Kammi cuts into her crepes and looks at me. Maybe she's judging whether the beach with me is a good alternative to art lessons. Or maybe she's thinking about what happened and whether being with me will cost her another chance to talk to Mother.

I don't want to go, either, but I'd rather be away from the house. I don't want to listen to Mother's pacing in her studio, or catch the smell of paint thinner creeping downstairs like a poisonous gas.

"A hat, too." Martia has found a straw hat somewhere. As we stand in the shade of the porch, she places the hat on Kammi's head, frames her face with it, and pushes the brim down. That way the sun can't find Kammi's fair skin so easily, but then she can't see very far ahead, either.

All I can see of her face is a nose dabbed with zinc oxide. She walks with the brim angled low, so she can see the ground just in front of her. A pad of heavy paper sticks out of her beach bag. From the rattling sound, I know there's a tin of drawing pencils in there, too.

I'm weighted down with the ice chest, the sun tent, and my own towel.

Kammi trudges behind me, the wind snatching away the sound of her sandals flapping against the soles of her feet. When we pass the boathouse, I know without looking that she has stopped in front of it. I keep going. If I don't look back, I can count on her following me like a puppy.

At the far end of the beach, just around the curve where Mother can no longer see us, even with binoculars, I stop. I turn around. Sure enough, Kammi's following me, and I wait for her to catch up.

CHAPTER EIGHT

WHEN KAMMI reaches me, she says, "I want to paint that boat." The wind flips her cover-up across her thighs. Her straw hat threatens to fly away, and she forces it down on her head.

I know the boat she means. I ignore her.

"This is just the shade of blue," she says, holding up a watercolor pencil in her fist, not giving up.

"No, it isn't." Her pencil is delft blue. The blue of the boat is more vibrant, richer in tone. More like ultramarine. The name even sounds like it should mean the ultimate or the perfect sea, but it doesn't. To medieval Italians, *oltramarino* meant "from beyond the seas." Maybe that's more accurate. A blue not of this world.

"Come on, it's farther." I start to walk again.

"How much farther?"

"The next beach over. Not far." We cut across inland through scrub and cacti. Lizard tracks weave through the hot sand. I like the way the heat feels, the way it sinks over my head, anchoring me to the ground. Kammi falls behind, the art supply bag over her shoulder. At least she's given up on the leather shoes and opted for plastic beach slides.

Down a long hill, the path opens up to another beach, a tucked-away cove. Too shallow for most boats, Boca Roja invites only swimmers who walk from the road at the top of the hill, or people who come from the grand houses, like the one we rent, along the shore. At dawn and dusk, the light here is almost reddish. I'm not sure why, whether it's the slant of the sun or some base color under the sand that comes out only at the ends of day. The full sun bleaches everything out.

We're the only beachgoers today. I pick a spot and start pounding stakes into the sand, the mallet making a hollow sound as it strikes.

"It is too the right color." Kammi doesn't give up. She plops down on her bottom on a red beach towel like a two-year-old child would. "It's just this shade."

"The light in the boathouse is no good." The mallet strikes until the wood sinks into the sand, and I fight to put up the tent. The loose fabric flaps in the wind like a flock of silk saris, the kind Mrs. Bindas's servants hang on the line by their beach. The saris catch the breeze and dry in under an hour. Not enough time to fade, she said once to Mother when they stood talking at the farm market. Mrs. Bindas held an armful of mangoes and Mother a clutch of watercolor pencils she'd brought to match the colors in the market.

"They smell so fresh, like the sea," Mrs. Bindas said about the saris.

But the sea doesn't always smell fresh—sometimes it reeks of marine life stranded ashore by low tide, and it tastes like tears.

The salt air burns my eyes.

"But if we open the doors—"

"No." I wrap my hands around the cloth, squeeze. "Grab that end, will you?" Be useful, that's what I want to say. Why I don't, I'm not sure. Most of this past year I've said anything that popped into my head.

Kammi fights to hold on to a corner of the cloth, and I wrestle it into place. Now we have a four-foot square of shade between us to share.

While Kammi pulls out her art supplies, arranging the Caran d'Ache watercolor pencils, the kind Mother would buy, around the blanket like a color wheel, I stare at the sea. She opens the water bottle and pours some into a small cup. She settles herself, flips over a fresh sheet of drawing paper, and pauses. I sense her close her eyes, centering herself. Mother does that, too, like she would a yoga pose, a breathing exercise to push away distractions.

In the distance, a fishing boat, probably heading from Venezuela to the floating market at Otrobanda, chugs along.

The wavelike shape of the prow reminds me again of the boat in the boathouse. Kammi's too busy settling herself to see it, to notice it's like the other one, the one I won't let her draw.

"Since my dad's been gone," Kammi begins. She doesn't mention the divorce. She says "gone," almost as if it were a passive act. Something done to him, to her. She takes a deep breath. "Ever since then, it's just been Mom and me. Mom says she won't marry anyone else. She won't even date. I sort of thought . . . well, I sort of thought that meant he might come back, you know?" She looks at me from under the hat and tears start to well in her eyes.

I thought my dad would come back, too. Even after they found his body trapped in the netting. Even after the boat was hauled onto the sand and into the boathouse. I thought he'd just swim out of the sea and laugh at me for worrying. Water and sand would stream down his face and body, making unexpected sand castles at his feet.

I stare at the sea. It feels possible even now, though I know it can't happen.

"Last fall, Dad came down to Atlanta for parents' weekend," Kammi says. "He said he'd come all the way from Maine for me."

The sand shifts under my feet. "When?"

"October."

Last Columbus Day weekend, Mother attended the

opening of her retrospective in Atlanta. She hired a departmental graduate assistant—to house-sit, she said, but she really meant to babysit me. She called once and I listened in. Mother claimed the show was a bore and that no one really important was there and what should she expect from the South, after all. Laughter erupted in the background, as if she were at a reception or a restaurant. A man's voice chuckled into the receiver. I imagined wineglasses being topped off, hors d'oeuvres being whisked by on trays.

Kammi grips her pencil hard and squints at the blank paper.

In October, Mother was in Atlanta.

So was Howard, Kammi's father.

I close my eyes and listen to the sea. Only four months after Dad died. Maybe they'd even traveled together. The surf rolls onto shore, curling as it comes, echoing in ripples down the beach. Mother didn't mention Howard until January. If she didn't mention him in October, does that mean she was seeing him even before Dad died? Was she having an affair?

Kammi turns to a fresh piece of paper even though she hasn't drawn anything on the first sheet, as if it was ruined before she started. "When Dad came, he brought me a gift from your mother. A tablet and some watercolor pencils. Caran d'Ache aquarelles. All because Dad told her I wanted to learn to paint. See?" She holds up her fresh pencils for me to see and I inhale the scent of new wood.

Aquarelles. Back in Maine, I have a tin of those, too, the tips still newly sharpened. Mother gave them to me as a gift in honor of her retrospective. She must have bought them at the same time she bought Kammi's, though she said nothing. It was the first art-related gift she'd given me since I was small. I didn't want the pencils. Still, I stashed the tin on a shelf in the back of the closet, because, despite everything, I couldn't bear to throw them away.

CHAPTER NINE

AFTER WE trudge back with our empty water bottle and sandy towels, I go to my room and close the door. Here in the back room, the walls are pale green. Until this year, I didn't know that this is the coolest room in the house. It keeps out the heat even on the hottest days. Martia said the owner wanted a room to remind him of Holland in the spring. Not the green-gray cold days that spit drizzle until June, but the green of tulip leaves emerging from the ground.

I open the glass box that I keep on my dresser and run my fingers through the small bits of sea glass I've gathered on the beach this summer—all but the largest piece, the one I'm saving for something special. That's inside the toe of an old sock I found in the back of the dresser when I moved in. Someone's lost sock. No one will look inside it, tucked there in plain view among my underwear.

Someone taps on my door. The sound isn't Mother's crisp knock, so I open it.

Kammi's changed out of her suit into a bandana dress. Squares of red fabric drape in a handkerchief hem. Her small red leather shoes remind me of Dorothy's from *The Wizard of Oz*, only these don't glitter.

"May I come in?" she asks as she peers over the lid of the glass box.

I back away from the door and she tiptoes inside. She slips onto the edge of my bed and looks everything over, not just the box I'm still holding, seeing it all for the first time. The green walls, the bookcase with a few dog-eared paperbacks, a few written in Dutch, left by previous guests. I've hidden *The History of Language* by covering it in a book jacket to hide the spine. The death certificate is in an envelope taped inside the back.

After Dad's death, the police commissioner didn't ask about what he might have been reading, and Mother didn't mention the book. Neither did I, though I recalled having seen it the day before he disappeared. First on his nightstand, where he'd sent me to fetch his reading glasses; later in a stack of magazines in the living room. It had been sandwiched between *Illumination*, an art magazine that Mother had read on the plane ride down, and *En Huis*. Martia scours the Dutch magazine cover to cover, admiring the neatly tiled houses of Holland but not the Europeans who come to Curaçao to spend their money and make fun of the locals. After Dr. Bindas returned the book, I kept thinking it might contain clues about what happened to Dad. There was an inscription inside, dated two years ago now, in Rome: "The history of language is the history of love." No signature. No initials, even. Maybe Dad had bought it used. As a professor, he often ordered secondhand books for research. This book seemed new, though, the spine barely creased, despite water damage to the cover.

"What's in there?" Kammi asks, nodding at the box.

"Sea glass. Mermaids' tears," I blurt out without thinking.

"Mermaids' tears?" Her eyes go big, as if perhaps she thinks I really believe in mermaids.

"It's just trash. Glass that's been tossed into the sea. I collect it."

"To do what with?"

I snap the lid shut. I'm not ready to tell Kammi how I make jewelry with it. I'm not ready to trust her with anything.

"Okay," she says, not asking me again. She looks around the room, maybe looking for clues about me. But there's not much here to see.

Finally, Kammi says: "Your mother's going to take me painting with her tomorrow." She says it casually, but I hear an edge to her voice.

"She asked you?"

"Yes, well, not exactly," Kammi says. She sits on her hands on my bed. "I was talking to her about the pencils, telling her I liked them. How I wanted to try watercolor. Dad thinks watercolor is the best."

"She didn't say draw first?" *Draw first* is Mother's mantra. Even Mother's star student, Philippa, had to prove her range of drawing skills before she graduated to paints.

"No. She's taking me to paint en plein air."

I know better. It's an old trick. Kammi doesn't realize that this trip with Mother isn't really about her going. It's about Mother getting someone to carry her supplies and trail at her feet like a servant. Maybe Mother wants a student, even if relationships with her students usually end after a couple of years, for different reasons.

Kammi will sit in the sun and burn if she forgets her sunscreen. The backs of her thighs will stick with sweat to the plastic webbed lawn chair that she'll have to carry. She'll sit there and Mother won't want Kammi to look at what she's doing because it's a work in progress. Even if there's nothing on the canvas. Mother might reach over once or twice and dab some paint on Kammi's paper to make it look like she's helping her.

I don't warn Kammi. She wouldn't believe me. She'd think I'm just feeling sour grapes, that I hate her because she's here, because my mother sent her watercolor pencils before I knew she even existed. Because Howard's coming to take

Dad's place. I don't hate her for all those reasons. I hate her because of the same gift of Caran d'Ache watercolor pencils stuffed into the back of my closet at home.

"Why don't you go with us?" Kammi asks me.

"Are you kidding?"

"You could."

"Why would I want to?"

Her shoulders relax and she smiles, her even white teeth showing. She wants Mother all for herself, but she can't help being polite enough to ask me to come along.

"Don't you paint?" she asks. Now that it's safe, now that I have told her I don't want to compete with her for Mother's attention, she asks the important question.

"No. I used to." The same way that I no longer swim, I don't paint or draw.

Kammi waits a minute. Maybe she thinks I'll say more, but I stand silent, holding the glass box, with my back against the bookcase. She doesn't ask why I don't paint. Maybe she's afraid my answer is like an illness that will infect her, too, and she won't be able to learn to paint and please her dad.

Finally, when I continue to stand mute, she slips off the bed and tiptoes out again.

After she leaves, I return the box to its place on the dresser and lie on my bed, staring at the ceiling. Suddenly, I feel tired from the heat outside. In my pocket, I feel for the Prussian blue oil paint that I took from Mother's studio. The cool metal edge curls where Mother has rolled up the end like a toothpaste tube, squeezing out the dark blue paint in small smudges against her palette. I should have hidden it by now, but I like the cool feel of it in my pocket. Prussian blue was developed in the sixteen hundreds. It became favored among artists because it didn't fade like indigo, and it cost less than cobalt.

When I was little, I pretended to be an artist like my mother. On Christmas Eve when I was seven, my grand-mother on my mother's side gave me dough she made herself with salt and flour. I cut out bell shapes with cookie cutters and we baked them while Mother painted in her studio. Back then, she had a studio at the university, and we lived in an apartment on campus. The ornaments smelled like bread coming out of the oven. After they cooled, Grandmother Betts let me decorate them with thick paint in red, blue, and yellow—primary colors—with a set of paints she'd bought just for me. We hung the ornaments that evening. When Mother got home, she said they smelled up the house and that I was too young to handle paints. Grandmother's voice got tinny and cold, but she didn't get into an argument. After Epiphany, after Grandmother had returned to her winter re-treat in Florida, Mother threw out the dough ornaments along with the tree. From the frosted window, I watched Dad haul it down to the curb on a Thursday when the garbage men were coming to truck away all the dead trees. When I cried and asked why, Mother said the ornaments wouldn't keep; they'd mold. My grandmother had said art was for children. But dough ornaments weren't even art, Mother said.

After Dad died last summer, I found one of the ornaments, a blue bell, in a pin box in his sock drawer at home. Bits of it had crumbled off, but I knew what it was. It still smelled clean, like salt. I hid the box from Mother before she cleared out his things.

I don't know why Dad kept that blue bell. Besides books, he saved little—his grandfather's hammer, his mother's wedding band after she died when I was eight, and an oil painting barely bigger than two inches square, with a scene of a gondola, a bridge, and clothes hanging on a line across a canal. He and Mother went to Venice on their honeymoon, so I assumed Mother had painted it herself. But when I held the small square frame to the Maine light, I saw the name Giuseppe along the edge. Someone else, not Mother, had painted it. So why did Dad keep it? What about Venice had stayed with him?

I want to ask him those questions. But now I will never know.

CHAPTER TEN

THE NEXT MORNING, Martia knocks on my door—I know it's Martia because she taps in a special rhythm—two short raps, a pause, and two more raps. I pull my fingers through my tangled hair. Last night I changed into a fresh T-shirt from my suitcase. It still holds the scent of the dryer sheets we use in Maine.

When I open the door, Martia motions for me to follow her. Intrigued, I tiptoe after her. Her skirt and blouse smell as fresh as sunshine. Martia doesn't believe that we should use electric dryers for our clothes, not when the sun is "for free." But how can I explain Maine to her? How the damp gray air almost never dries out?

Martia knocks gently on Kammi's door. Kammi opens it, grinning. Just like the first afternoon when we walked over to the Bindases' house, she's polished and ready to go, even down to her plastic slides. She's hidden her hair under a bandana. This time, she looks the part of an artist. I can see her as a model for the front of an art-school brochure. All she's missing is a smudge of blue paint on her nose for effect.

"I come in? Yes?" Martia asks. "Cyan, too?"

Kammi nods. Her eyebrows lower when she looks past Martia at me. She backs away to let us both in. Martia stands just inside the door, and I slip behind her into the room that every year before this one has been mine.

"I come to explain," Martia says, and she folds her hands gently in front of her, as if she is about to take the wafer from the priest at Communion. "Mrs. Walters, she can no paint in the air today." Martia calls en plein air "in the air." I imagine artists weightless, suspended in midair, painting on floating canvases.

"What do you mean?" Kammi's face clouds. "Is she sick?"

Martia nods. "A headache. *Mala cabeza.* Mrs. Walters, she no go out today. I call Jinco already. He take you to Willemstad. Be tourists today, yes? Much better idea. Mrs. Walters has left some money for you to spend."

Martia asks it as a question of Kammi, but it isn't. Be good girls and go into town and leave Mrs. Walters to recover. Don't make a scene. I tilt my head back, imagine Mother lying above us in her bed in her studio, her eyes squeezed shut against the light that almost won't be kept out up there. She should be in my room, tucked against the back of the house in the cool green shadows. But down here is too close to her old room, the closed-off room she shared with my father when he came to the island.

I savor the taste of Kammi's disappointment. She doesn't cry or stamp her foot, but she looks at me sharply. Maybe she thinks it's my fault, that I did something to make Mother come down with a headache.

I shrug as if she's asked me a question out loud. Who knows? Maybe Mother doesn't really have a headache. Maybe she doesn't want to paint en plein air with a beginner, one who will look at her as if she's a goddess. Maybe it makes her uncomfortable, though that's hard to imagine, given the way Philippa used to hang around our house near the lake. She started out following ten paces behind Mother wherever she went, until she became more skilled herself. After a while, Philippa became an artist in her own right. Then she started to walk beside Mother, as if they were equals.

"Okay," Kammi says, lowering her eyes. "If I can't paint today, going to town will be okay."

Other than the day we arrived at the airport, I haven't been to Willemstad this year. It's my chance to take the sea glass I've collected so far to the bead shop to sell.

"Another day, you paint with Mrs. Walters. It is no problem." Martia smiles and straightens the small silver pin, shaped like a palette, on Kammi's blouse. No doubt she is wearing a gift from her grandmother. Only a grandmother would give that pin to anyone who truly wanted to be an artist.

Kammi smiles and Martia hugs her. I slip money from Martia's outstretched hand into my pocket.

Jinco looks in his rearview mirror when he should be watching the shell road twist and turn in front of the cab. He pretends he's looking at me, but he's staring at Kammi, because all the men will gaze at her in the way they're not supposed to, eyes turned away yet studying her sideways. She's just a child, they'll think. They'll be right, but Kammi already has a sexy look, whether she knows it or not.

I stare down Jinco when he looks my way. He remembers last year, I know, but he still showed up to meet us at the airport this year, as if this were just another summer and Dad was staying in Maine like he often did. Dad would say he shouldn't interfere, that Mother had to have her space. And her space didn't always include him. Maybe it didn't always include me, either. But she always brought me to the island. I came along like a barnacle attached to the hull of a sleek speedboat.

In Willemstad, Jinco jerks the cab to a stop near a banyan tree before the Queen Emma pontoon bridge.

"We'll meet you here at four o'clock," I say. In the heat of the afternoon. I'm probably making him come for us just when he'd be taking a nap under a shade tree or having a beer.

Jinco shrugs and taps the car clock, the one that runs ten minutes slow compared to my plastic wristwatch. "Four," he says. He'll be late. He and I both know it.

"Come on, get out on this side." I slide out the door and motion to Kammi to follow.

She says thank you to Jinco. His eyes follow her in the side-view mirror. He can't help himself.

When Jinco speeds off, leaving a cloud of burned oil in our faces, we're standing on the pontoon bridge. The Queen Emma Bridge opens to let the big cruise ships in and out of the main harbor. Every summer, I come down at least once to wave as the ships inch out of port, saying goodbye to tourists pointing their cameras at us from the deck.

I lean over the side. Anemones cling to the pontoons and the bridge supports near the shore. "If you squint, you can see through the water at an angle."

Kammi stares, a few strands of hair blowing across her face.

"There," I say, pointing. "Just on the edge, see the parrotfish?"

Her gaze darts back and forth along the water. I can tell she can't see it.

"Look *through* the water. Follow the light." I point again. "Quick, before a cloud moves in front of the sun." The fish hovers just there, motionless.

Kammi throws out her arm, pointing. "I see it."

Looking where her hand is pointing, I see nothing. The startled fish has moved away.

"Sure," I say. Whatever. "Come on." We pass the tourist shops closest to the cruise-ship dock, the ones that pay extra so they can be listed in the brochures. "Safe, friendly sales staff." "Air conditioning." "Extra-special prices," they claim, "just for the ship passengers." It's a lie. No one checks to see if I'm with a cruise ship when I claim a discount. Maybe they mumble, "Ship?" and I name whatever ship is in port. Only once last year, a nosy clerk, just a little older than me, asked me for my ship card, for proof, and she thought she had me. Her smirk and unbelieving eyes said so. I shrugged and claimed my mother had my ID card. Then I said loudly, so the manager would hear, "She's not coming to this shop, so I guess there's no sale." The girl gave in and sold me the shell bracelets for ten percent off. Better a sale than no sale, and no skin off her nose if I cheated the owner. She'd have done the same. And the truth? The truth is the ten percent discount is no discount, but we all play the game.

Kammi darts under the shady overhang of a food stand, where the air smells of cinnamon, one of Curaçao's exports. An oscillating fan whips the scent into the air, and it wafts into the street, where it mingles with dust and diesel. Tourists slathered in sunscreen mill about, struggling behind tour guides with tasseled flagpoles, calling out for beach tour this and snorkeling tour that.

Kammi waits in line and buys a Coke with ice. She

hands over her money and then takes a second cup and passes it to me, without asking if I want one.

I can't be bought for a cold drink.

But I take it.

When the mob of cruise tourists pass, I lead us down a quiet side street. Colores. The shell and bead shop is still there. I feel the bulge of sea glass in my skirt pocket. I keep no valuables in the crocheted purse that hangs across my body, over my left shoulder. It dangles there, the button closure open, tempting pickpockets. It holds some small coins, a bandana, a map from the cruise ship that someone dropped and I scavenged.

A bell over the door tinkles as we enter Colores, barely noticeable above the clatter of the air conditioning. Kammi stands just inside the doorway, taking in the wooden bowls of beads covering every empty space. I felt the same way the first time I came here. It is too much—the colors, the textures, the promise.

At the first table, Kammi runs her fingers through blue glass beads.

"Like your sea glass," she says. She picks out an assortment of blue beads and bundles them into a small white envelope. Then she heads for the silver beads at a table across the room. She can see possibilities.

I turn away and hang out near the front counter, waiting for the owner to appear. Kammi's seen the sea glass in my room. Does she know I gather it every morning, early? The sea is my field. It decides whether to give up its treasures, whether to cast onto the beach shards of glass, worn smooth, for me to glean. I only keep the best blues.

"Do you have crimps, pliers?" Kammi asks. She's moved on to the shelves of tools and wire.

"Yes," I say from across the room. I pretend to look at beading magazines by the checkout. I don't want her to see my sale. Mother doesn't know about the sea glass. I didn't even pack pliers. But I left an old, cheap set of tools that Martia knows about in the storage area under the deck. Some silver wire, too, in a velvet pouch. It's probably all tarnished now, since it's been a year.

"Beading thread?"

I nod. A spool should be there. I look over leaflets for beading classes being held here on the days the cruise ships dock in port. For tourists again. The door opens, and three cruise-ship tourists—I can tell from their shoulder totes labeled with the ship's name—waddle in, out of the heat.

Kammi wanders down another aisle of wooden dishes teasing her with beads—glass, coral, wood, even plastic, like the beads they throw to tourists in New Orleans during Mardi Gras.

The owner, Antje, appears from the back room, her thighs swishing together under a wide-banded skirt. She's come out because of the tourists, who laugh and joke with each other about who makes the best necklaces back home in New Jersey. When Antje sees me, she motions with her hand, pats the barest space of counter, as though I haven't been gone a year.

From the pocket in my skirt, I take out a plastic bag of small bits of sea glass, spilling them onto the wooden counter. Antje squints and runs her hands over each piece, as if she can tell by touch whether they're fake, whether they're from this island. Or if they're tumbled by machine rather than by the ocean. The artist who buys them from her wants only local glass—she says it evokes the mystery of the island. It costs more, too, the shop owner knows. In exchange for the glass, Antje counts out small bills and square coins for me. She slips them into a white paper envelope as if they're beads I'm purchasing. In case the taxman comes snooping, she says.

I look over my shoulder. Kammi is distracted by the boxes of Venetian glass beads, these and the tourists exclaiming all around her about the spiraling blown glass. She doesn't even notice my transaction.

My secret is safe.

CHAPTER ELEVEN

K AMMI AND I leave Antje cajoling the tourists, trying to sell them Chinese beads at European prices. Outside, I breathe in the heat and blink at the brightness.

"Let's go this way," I say, pointing away from the shopping district.

"Okay," Kammi agrees, following me. Not questioning.

I've been thinking about the commissioner's letter, how the report is final and sealed away forever. To me, though, it's like a scab, healed over only on the outside. Underneath the wound is still raw, with too many questions left unanswered.

Maybe the commissioner knows Mayur's cousin. Maybe I can find him here. I can confront him myself to see what he knows. Then I won't have to give Mayur the satisfaction of holding something over me until I beg him to tell me.

I lead us to the shell-white building with the flag out front.

"Let's go in," I say.

"What's this?"

"It's where the commissioner's office is."

"What are we going to do here?" Kammi gives me a frown.

"I just have a question."

Kammi doesn't move forward when I begin to climb the steps.

"I don't think I'll go in," she says.

"Okay. Just wait here. I don't want to have to tell Mother I lost you." I don't wait to see what she does.

At the top I push through the door. A guard stands at the entrance. He leans against the counter with the hip that doesn't have a sidearm buckled to it. A fan in the corner turns, washing cool air over me as it moves back and forth. The movement of air riffles papers on the counter.

"Office is now closed."

I should have thought of that. Some things close here in the heat of the day. Only shops that cater to tourists are busy now. Everyone else goes in search of shade and a quiet place until later in the afternoon.

"It's important. I need to see Mr. Botha. The commissioner?" I stand up tall, trying to look important, imperious, the way Mother would if she wanted something here. This guard won't ask me questions if I act like my mother.

He frowns. "Mr. Botha is not here. The commissioner is Mr. Pieter Drak now. Mr. Botha, he is gone. Retired. Sorry." The guard's lips turn down, as if he really is sad that he can't make the commissioner—the old commissioner—appear. "Perhaps Mr. Drak, he can help you. Later?"

I shake my head. A new commissioner wouldn't know.

How could Mr. Botha retire? He has an unsolved case. In the United States, the police don't give up. They keep cold cases going for years. I hear about them all the time, the unsolved cases closed with the discovery of only a small bit of evidence. Maybe something as small as a chip of blue paint.

The guard hands me a card. "Here, here is the number. If you change your mind." I pocket Mr. Drak's card.

"How about Dr. Bindas? Do you know him?" If the guard knows Dr. Bindas, then he might know the cousin who works in the government.

Again, he shakes his head. "No."

Disappointed, I find Kammi outside on the stairs in the shade thrown by the building across the street. She's sitting with her back to me.

I plop down beside her.

"Did you find out something?" she asks.

"Nothing."

"What were you going to ask? Is it about the letter your mother got?"

"Yes," I say. "It's about my father."

Kammi opens her mouth and then closes it again, as if she's

thought better of asking a question she might not want to know the answer to. Dad wasn't part of the reason she came here. After all, Dad is gone. Her father is moving into the picture.

I squint at the clock tower across the street. "Come on. Jinco will be here soon."

Near the cruise-ship dock, we buy cold drinks and sit on a bench underneath a tree. I watch a pair of lizards chase each other along the wall. Sunburned tourists, laden with shopping bags, head back to the ship like lemmings.

When Jinco shows up, he makes a big show, driving a huge circle around us and doubling back, crossing in front of three small cars, all missing something: a bumper, a radio antenna, a side mirror. Men drinking at the café bar wave noisily, yipping their appreciation. At his driving, or at Kammi. Or maybe both. She and I spill into the back seat. As he takes the curve again to more hoots of pleasure, we slosh into each other like waves.

Kammi leans over to me. "Is he drunk?"

I look at Jinco's eyes in the rearview mirror.

"No. He's just showing off." At that, Jinco settles back into being Jinco the taxi driver for expats and tourists, the safe driver, one a mother would be comfortable leaving her daughter and daughter-to-be with for an afternoon.

"Why don't you drive us to Santa Catarina? To the ostrich farm? We have time."

Jinco takes his foot off the gas. A minibus rattles past, nearly running a Jeep off the road coming the other way. Jinco ignores the traffic. "Go there now? Martia, she pay me for roundtrip to Willemstad. That's all she pay."

I take bills from my pocket. "I'll pay extra." I'm in no rush to go home, to see if Mother has recovered from her headache. Though I don't want to make Martia wait, we have time enough to drive by and feed the ostriches. In the early years that Dad came, he liked to take me to feed them. He watched the birds, their blinking eyes and long eyelashes. "Intelligent birds," he said. "You can see it in their eyes." Mother never came, claimed she was allergic to feathers. One year, Dad bought me a hollowed ostrich egg, the blue color just for me, he said. Some of the eggs were sold with painted designs on them, but I liked the plain ones. Holding them up to the light, I could see the pale inner wall, how the blue color bleeds through to the creamy underside.

Jinco nods curtly. He's made up his mind. He brakes, then yanks the wheel and heads back to the cutoff. He makes a hard right turn and we're off, speeding past a bus and a truck sagging with water bottles.

By the time we get there, Kammi has her face pressed to the window, watching the fields for ostriches. Jinco stops the car at the entrance.

"I wait here," he says, motioning to a tree where a minibus is pulling away. The shady spots are so few in this area, he needs to stake out one for himself. Tour buses have lined up farther along the gate and driveway. He points at his car clock. "Thirty minutes. Then we go. My day, it is finish."

Jinco is lying. He's waiting to go back into town and drive drunk late-afternoon tourists back to the cruise ship before it sets sail at dusk. He can charge extra. Martia says he makes good money on ship days. She had to pay him extra out of Mother's stash just to ensure he'd take us out today, at the last minute. I heard her negotiating with him.

"Come on." Jinco knows I heard him. This is my game.

I make a show of paying for Kammi at the gate. It's the money Martia pressed into my hands as she sent us off this morning. But Kammi doesn't know that. Maybe she thinks I'm being nice.

The staff lets us feed a baby ostrich. Kammi stretches out her hand, and the bird's long neck curves over as it takes some pellets in its beak, carefully, as if it's been trained.

"Does your mother ever come here?" Kammi asks.

"My mother?"

"Yes, does she?"

"No. She doesn't. She doesn't like animals. Why do you care?"

Kammi pulls her hand back and pours more pellets into it from the plastic container. The ostrich stares at her hand, then pecks more food. Kammi holds her arm steady. She doesn't even blink when the ostrich's beak taps her palm. "I want her to like me." She says it fiercely.

"Why? She's going to be your stepmother. Don't you believe all those tales about stepmothers?"

"No. Dad said—"

"Do you do everything he wants you to do?"

"No."

"I bet you do. *Dad* wants you to paint with watercolors. *Dad* wants you to get along with my mother. Did he tell you to be nice to me, too?"

Kammi blushes. "He said I couldn't win you over. He said I shouldn't try."

I laugh. "But you are trying."

Kammi doesn't look at me, but the ostrich turns to me and blinks. I don't know if my dad was right about ostriches. This bird looks pretty stupid to me. It listens to my voice, cocks its head, as if trying to figure out what laughter is about. Then it pecks at Kammi's empty palm, searching for more. She snatches her hand away. If ostriches are so smart, like Dad said, it should go straight for the plastic bin where the pellets are stored and not look for handouts from strangers.

CHAPTER TWELVE

MARTIA OPENS the door for us before Jinco has even driven away. She's been waiting, keeping dinner warm. Kammi goes straight to her room. I wait in the hallway as Martia tiptoes up the metal stairs to Mother's studio and knocks. The door opens, closes. I listen but I can't hear anything.

I'm the first to sit at the table. From here I can see the mail Martia has stacked on the sideboard. Facing me is a postcard. I reach over and pick it up. The scene is familiar. Ponte dei Sospiri. Bridge of Sighs, Venice. Only this isn't just a postcard. It's a print of a painting of the famous landmark at dusk. I can make out the shadow of a gondola going under the bridge, away from the artist. A grayish, ghostly couple sits in front of the gondolier, facing forward. The postcard reminds me of another gondola—the small framed painting in Dad's drawer.

I turn the card over. The loopy handwriting addressing the card to Mother in care of the Dutch owner looks familiar. Philippa. Postmarked from Italy. I can't help reading it. She writes that she painted the scene and made it into postcards for souvenir shops. She's won a commission to paint all the major bridges of Venice. She writes that it's good luck for a couple to sail under the Bridge of Sighs.

Kammi wanders into the room, scoots her chair close to the table at the far end, and stares at her plate. She hasn't said anything to me since the ostrich farm. Maybe I hurt her feelings. I'm not sorry if I did.

Mother comes downstairs slowly, too, as if she still has a headache and the echo of her footsteps on the metal staircase sounds loud to her own ears.

"What's that?" she asks.

"A postcard. You'll never believe who it's from."

Mother looks pale. "I don't feel like playing a game, Cyan. Just give me the card."

I hold it up for her to see the front. Kammi, too.

"Recognize it? It's Venice. Know anyone there?" I ask.

Mother stares at the picture.

"Give up?" I ask. "It's from Philippa."

"Who's that?" Kammi asks.

"One of Mother's best art students. Her last one, actually," I answer. "Isn't that right, Mother?"

"Yes," Mother says, then presses her lips together in a thin line.

"Philippa says she has a commission to paint the most famous bridges in Venice. This is her first one, the Bridge of Sighs."

"I've heard of that bridge," Kammi says, smiling.

"Please put it away, Cyan. I'd like to eat in peace." Mother unfolds her napkin. That's Martia's signal to serve.

Martia moves efficiently between the kitchen and the table. She places a salad next to Kammi and a pitcher of iced tea next to me. Then she uses both hands to carry in a steaming bowl of saffron rice and shellfish. She nestles it right in front of Mother, the steam rising into Mother's face.

"*Kome, kome,*" Martia pleads with us as she reties her apron. "Eat, eat."

Kammi picks at her salad, not bothering to arrange the greenery, the way she did her first day. Today she is more abstract expressionist, like Jackson Pollock, jumbling the vegetables on her plate, not caring how they're placed. She's not trying to please the eye. All because I got her to say what Howard said about me? And I laughed at her? Or because Mother ignored her when she said she knew about the Bridge of Sighs?

I fish out some carrots and red cabbage from the salad bowl Kammi passes to me before sliding it across the table to Mother, who doesn't even seem to notice. She's too busy scooping rice in slow motion. I like the colors that clash on my plate. When Mother passes the rice dish, I'll spoon yellow rice and pink shrimp onto my palette, too.

"Do you have a student now?" Kammi asks.

"No," I answer for Mother.

"Cyan, I can answer for myself," Mother says. "Kammi, having a student is a big investment. At the moment, I'm trying to concentrate on my own work."

Kammi looks crestfallen.

I smirk into my napkin. Kammi's dreaming if she thinks Mother will take her on. Kammi, whose only painting experience is grade school art once a week. This week, bringing Kammi to Curaçao into Mother's sanctuary, this is just for show. Just to make a good impression for Howard's benefit.

Mother takes a long drink of iced tea, reviving herself. She asks, "Kammi, what'd you think of Willemstad?"

"I liked it. We walked along the floating market. We also went to a bead store. It had interesting beads, more than I've seen at home."

I breathe in and out. Tingling with almost-fear that she'll mention the commissioner. Anticipating Mother's reaction.

"Do you string beads?" Mother sounds as though she's trying to make up to Kammi for the lost day. She plants her elbows on the table and holds her head in her left hand. With her free hand, she stirs the saffron rice around on her plate, placing the shellfish on top of the rice haystacks. Mother thinks stringing beads is like painting by numbers.

Or knitting from a pattern. It's just a craft. It isn't Art. I've heard her say it enough.

"Beading's something I can do with my friends." Here, Kammi looks at me. She must be thinking of how things might have been different, how we could have shared beading together. I can tell just by the way she said "friends."

"Antje has classes, all on cruise-ship days. I bet you could take one next week." Smiling, I offer the classes up to her. She'll think I'm being kind. Mother might suspect I'm not, since I know how she feels about bead stringing. When I took a beading class last summer after we went home to Maine, Mother encouraged it only because it meant I wasn't eating and I wasn't moping around the house, disturbing her studio time. She never asked to see my work. She didn't even know that what I liked was wire-working in silver. The beads almost didn't matter, and stringing them on fine, nearly invisible thread bored me. But the silver I liked. I liked the feel of it in my hand, the way the warmth of my fingers softened the wire and allowed it to be shaped, capturing blown-glass beads, making three-dimensional sculpture on a small scale. It made me think for the first time that I might someday feel better again. Because at least in those moments, I forgot that Dad had died. I forgot that I felt mostly nothing.

I gave most of it away. I saved only one piece, and it isn't finished. It's silver with blue sea glass. I don't have enough sea glass yet to finish it.

"I'm sure Kammi can take bead classes back in Atlanta."
Bead stores are the latest fad, she's thinking, I know.

Kammi's bottom lip sags.

"What else did you do?" Mother asks her. "Something unique to Curaçao, I hope."

Kammi picks at her rice. She cuts her eyes at me. "The ostrich farm," she says in a whisper, maybe uncertain what to say next, whether Mother approves.

Mother frowns at me. "Ostrich farm? You had time to go there?"

"Jinco said he'd take us," I say.

Martia swishes around the table, clucking at the lack of food being consumed by everyone but me. That and she's probably disapproving of the detour to the ostrich farm. She'd know I would have had to bribe Jinco to take us, which made us late coming back. On purpose. And it cost more money.

"You liked it?" Mother sounds accusing when she asks Kammi, but she smiles at the end of the sentence, as if she's sorry she's said the words but they're out.

Kammi folds her hands in front of her plate. "A little." A weaselly answer. She should have just said yes in a loud voice. Or even no because the ostrich scared her, or because I was mean, or because feathers make her sneeze.

"Tomorrow I'll take you painting, like I planned for today. Just the two of us." Mother raises her head off her hand, sits straighter. She takes pity on Kammi. "That's more fun than any old petting zoo. I'm feeling much better."

"It's not a petting zoo," I say. On the refrigerated shelves at the farm store, tourists can buy ostrich meat. Hardly what they'd sell at a petting zoo in the United States. The signs say "Ostrich: leaner than beef, lower in cholesterol." I'm surprised Mother doesn't buy it for me.

Mother doesn't respond to my comment.

I feel the postcard in my lap. For the moment, Mother has forgotten it. Eventually, she'll ask for it. She'll say she's glad for Philippa. She'll be lying. Something happened between Mother and her best student; what, I don't know. Mother doesn't want competition in her art, I know that.

I'd like to lie, too, and say everything between us will be okay. If I lie, then maybe we can pretend we remember the same things. Like the article that came out the day after Dad died. It said the boat was gray. But the boat was blue. The paper said his body was found washed ashore. But he was found trapped in fish netting, one end of the rope still tied to the boat.

CHAPTER THIRTEEN

GOING TO PAINT en plein air the next morning is a production. Mother is late because one of her precious tubes of oil paint is missing. (I wonder which one it could be.) When she finally arrives downstairs, Martia scurries around to pack a soft-sided cooler with drinks while Mother collapses her field easel. An art bin holding her oil paints teeters on the edge of the counter. She's armed to do battle with the elements that defy the artist. The wind that carries with it bits of sand, which stick to still-wet canvases.

I sit at the kitchen table, pretending to read one of Kammi's stupid horse books. Kammi stands half in and half out of the room. She looks as if she thinks she's supposed to be doing something to help but no one has told her what to do.

Dressed in a pale pink linen shorts set, she looks ready for a garden party, complete with gardenia scent.

She'll find out soon enough what she's supposed to do. Beast of burden.

Martia draws her in. "Sit, sit. All is no problem. All is well." Kammi lets herself be coaxed into the kitchen to perch on the edge of a chair, ready to go at Mother's call.

Mother wears a flimsy metallic cover-up over her one-piece. "Don't you look nice," she says to Kammi.

Then she slaps a wide-brimmed straw hat onto her artist case.

"You've been out?" Mother nods at the bottom of my skirt, damp and sandy.

"Walking. You said exercise is better than Ding Dongs and Ho Hos."

Kammi blushes and stares at the floor. Maybe she's embarrassed on my behalf, because she's thin and I'm not.

Mother brushes air away as if she's walked into a spider web. "What are you going to do?" she asks.

"Besides read?" I lift the book.

Mother doesn't lose it. "While Kammi and I are painting." Mother smiles at Kammi, sharing a secret with a fellow artist.

I think of all the things I might say. Write to Zoe, help Martia in the kitchen. Sand the blue boat, or touch up the scratches along the underside, the scratches that couldn't be seen until the boat was lifted out of the water.

I shrug. It doesn't matter.

"Do something productive. I don't want to find you just lying around when we get back."

I bury myself in the sentences of the book until I hear them leave. Then I fold the corner of the page and crease it.

The house becomes silent, but then Martia starts making a racket in the kitchen, washing the dishes, banging pots, chopping vegetables for the next meal. She saves her fury for the kitchen. I wander outside onto the veranda, clutching Kammi's stupid novel. I'm not reading it, it's just a prop.

The stiff breeze shudders along the veranda, whipping my hair and the flag hanging from the widow's walk.

After a few minutes, I meander into the kitchen and filch a coconut cookie off a plate. Martia smiles, shaking her head at the same time. When I go out again, she's still working.

Mother's studio.

I leave Kammi's novel on the glass table in the living room. Open, spine up, as if I've walked out of the room for another cookie but am coming right back to pick up where I left off.

Barefoot, I don't make a sound even on the metal stairs. The scarf around my neck bounces down my back as I skip the third stair from the top because it creaks.

Mother's room smells of paint thinner, almost of pine. More Maine than Curaçao. The easel faces the back wall. I hold my breath and walk in front of it.

Paint clings to the canvas, a light wash of color. The pencil lines show through, giving guidelines for the next step.

The outline of a boat on the water. It's hard to tell if it is *the* boat. Whether she will actually dare to paint it.

But she is painting, or at least preparing to paint.

I flip open the tackle-box case that holds the paints she plans to use most for her current project. That's how she organizes her work. The ultramarine is on top. Ultramarine for the bold lines of the boat, to distinguish it from the water. To show the depth where the boat meets the waterline. It's the next color she'll apply.

From my pocket, I pull out the Prussian blue. I substitute it for the ultramarine in the tackle box and snap the lid shut. The ultramarine goes in my pocket, a new tube cold against my leg.

I go out through the doors and onto the widow's walk. From here, Mother must have seen Dad take the boat out. She must have stood here, watching the boat cut the swells until it merged with the sea and disappeared.

There was no storm that day, only calm seas. Clear skies. That first night, the stars shone until the light from the bonfires quenched them and they faded away.

At first, I thought he'd just left, taken the boat and returned to Willemstad by sea, to catch a ride to the airport. I told Mother to check the airport. Martia looked at me, as if she thought I understood something I wasn't supposed to. But Dad didn't lash the boat to the pier in Punda and take a flight out that night. When they checked the roster of outgoing flights the next day, his name wasn't on any of them. Mother told the commissioner, "It was a ridiculous idea." She folded her arms tightly around her middle. "I told you."

I'm sitting on the deck after lunch when I hear them returning. I stretch out the way Mother would if she wanted to look relaxed. It doesn't take long before the French doors snap open.

"Where is it?" Mother grips the doorframe as if to hold herself steady on a rolling ship.

Squinting, I turn toward her and pull my scarf in front of my face, making a gauzy film between Mother and me. "What?"

"Prussian blue. Winsor and Newton."

I smile. The Prussian is one of her most prized blues. I should have buried it in a tin box under the deck, like a treasure. The paints are evidence, after all, though not the kind the commissioner wanted when Dad died. Or I might have pitched the paint into the sea—but I couldn't. The color makes me ache, too. I'm ashamed that I can feel the way she does about anything.

"What are you talking about?" I ask. "We're not even allowed in your studio."

"There isn't a 'we' here. Don't bring Kammi into this." Mother shuts the French doors, keeping our argument away from her.

The sea gleams in the bright sun.

Whitecaps toss on the surface.

I pick up a pad of paper and a pencil from the wrought-iron deck table as if I'm an investigative reporter. "When's the last time you saw it?"

"You think this is funny?" Mother folds her arms in front of her, digging her nails into her skin. "Do you know how much Winsor and Newton costs? I can't get it here. I'll be stuck leaving that section undone until we get back to Maine."

I know how much it costs. Over the summers, I've been dragged by Mother to all the art supply stores, good and bad, in Willemstad. Most of what can be had is second rate, the tubes dried out, the colors unreliable. She'd never trust her blues to one of the local merchants. "So, you're painting again?"

"I am." Her tone says that she knows I've been in her studio.

"I'm so happy for you." I cover my head with the scarf. It shields the sides of my face like a prayer shawl, and the sunlight filters through it. I study the notebook in my hand, flip the pages. Tiny perfect squares of blue-lined graph paper blur as the pages cascade. "I should write that down." I'll keep a diary of my mother's special events. Someday, she'll want to write her memoir, and she'll want to know all the important dates. I'll be sure to underline June 23 several times so she won't forget it.

"Write what down?"

"The day you started painting again."

She glares at me.

"You write this down," Mother says. "'My mother knows I've been lying and stealing.'"

I laugh. "Strong words, Mother. 'Lie' and 'steal.' What have I stolen? What have I lied about?"

"Lied, past tense? You're still lying." Her face tightens. "The blue paint."

"When did you see it last?" I hold my pencil over the tiny boxes, touch the point to the inside of one, prepared to fill it in.

Mother doesn't answer.

"You should check your studio," I say. "You've probably just misplaced it." In my mind I see the Prussian blue safe in her tackle box, ready for the next project. When she finds it, she'll learn that another color is missing.

I can't get the view of the sea from the widow's walk out of my head. "Why did you let him go out alone?" I ask Mother. That day, Dad took a bucket of ice and a bottle of champagne with him. No champagne flutes were found on the boat—just some shards—but two wineglasses were missing from the house. Martia reported them lost to the commissioner when he came to interview her. Otherwise, the missing items would have been charged to her, the cost deducted from her wages.

"What do you mean?" Mother asks, stepping back.

"Dad. You should have gone with him."

"He liked fishing alone," Mother said.

"With champagne?"

"You think I knew about the champagne ahead of time?"

I don't answer her. I believe she did.

When she sees the expression on my face, she moves toward the door.

"You did know." It's not a question. Dad asked her to go out on the boat that day and she turned him down. That much I know. I overheard them by accident. What else did she say to him when she turned and left him standing there?

"I don't have to be interrogated by you."

"You knew Howard back in October. Before then, too, didn't you? Did you tell Dad about Howard?"

Her face goes slack. She opens her mouth, maybe to tell me something, something honest. But she doesn't speak. Her lips narrow, sealing her mouth closed.

"Did you tell the commissioner about Howard?" I ask.

Mother could tell me that Howard only came later, after Dad died, whether it's true or not. She could say that they got together only after Dad died and because she was lonely. She could say that's what she told the commissioner.

She doesn't.

The French doors slam shut.

CHAPTER FOURTEEN

KAMMI FINDS me lying on the sand underneath the deck, where I've retreated. From here, I can hear the ocean but I'm away from the light, from the sea breeze. Looking up through the slats, I see shadows crisscross over me. Kammi's standing in the sun, shading her eyes to look at me. Her head is covered by a straw hat, and I can see her zinc-oxide-tinted nose. She clutches a drawing pad to her chest.

"Why didn't you tell me?" she asks.

I roll onto my side to face her. "Tell you what?"

"About your dad."

"What about him?"

Kammi squeezes the drawing paper closer, like a shield. "My dad told me he died. But you should have told me about the boat—" She stops herself. "You should have told me the *way* he died. I made such a big deal about the boat. You could have warned me. I kept trying to get you to show me the boat."

I say nothing.

Her voice wobbles. "I said something about the boat to your mother."

I sit up. "You did? What'd she do?"

"She twisted around and knocked over her easel. Her painting ended up in the sand. I picked it up. I tried to brush the sand off. But everything smudged. It was supposed to be a harbor scene, with all the boats in the distance. It's ruined." Her voice rises at the end.

"Did you tell Mother it was ruined?" I try to imagine the scene, what happened, the melding of paints and sand.

Kammi's voice catches. "You should have told me. You knew I wanted to paint that boat." Tears glide down her face. "You did it on purpose. To make me look bad."

I stare at her. Her pretty pink skin appears blotchy, the way fair people get when they're upset. Their feelings erupt out of their skin like measles.

"My mother told me you'd be wicked," Kammi said. "She used just that word. 'Wicked.'"

I laugh. "Wicked" should hurt. "Why'd she say wicked? She doesn't even know me."

"She said you'd be angry about your mother marrying my

dad. That it was natural you'd be jealous." Kammi scratches her hands up and down the sketchpad.

I tie the scarf over my hair. "Jealous? That shows how stupid your mother is. Or maybe that's how she feels about it."

Kammi blinks.

"Jealousy would mean I care what my mother does," I say.

Kammi exhales hard. "You don't . . ."

"No. She can marry the man in the moon and live happily ever after." But there is no happily ever after. Not for her and Dad. Not even for her and Howard. Dad and I will always be between them.

Kammi stands there, staring at me as though I'm a strange lizard that slithered across the sand into the shade. I bet boarding school didn't prepare her for this, for a stepsister-to-be who isn't competition, someone who sidesteps all her thrusts.

"You didn't say why you didn't tell me." Kammi rubs at the tears and ends up smudging zinc oxide off part of her nose and onto her wet cheek. If it were a Prussian blue smudge, she'd seem more like an artist.

"I thought it best not to say anything."

Kammi holds the force field of drawing paper in front of her as she leaves.

I close my eyes, pull the scarf over my face. Through

the layers of cloth, the light is even dimmer when I open my eyes again. Two lizards circle each other along the retaining wall.

I think about Mother's easel collapsing into the sand, the gritty images forever marred. The Christmas after the episode with the salt-dough ornaments, my grandmother didn't come—she was too feeble—but she sent me a long box with an easel inside. The gift was for me, though Mother checked the label three times to make sure it was my name on front. She thought Grandmother Betts had made a mistake because of her growing dementia; she kept mixing up people's names and she did things like put her glasses instead of the juice bottle into the refrigerator.

Dad screwed together the easel parts, but one leg always seemed shorter than the others, and it tottered if I wasn't careful. I positioned the easel in my room so the light came through my window over my left shoulder. Between Christmas and New Year's, I splashed bold watercolor marks across the paper, just to see the colors tumble and blend. Mother didn't "interfere," as she called it, with the artistic process to tell me to work with form and shadow. She didn't tell me about the Golden Mean, the balance of the longer side of the image to the shorter. Or explain negative space. I either had talent or I didn't. She didn't want to encourage another artist. After New Year's, I folded the easel and put it away. Only a few spatters of blue paint like spilled sky still stained the carpet. Mother said, "It's good you quit so soon. Nana shouldn't have encouraged you. She never encouraged me."

Martia clambers down the stairs from the deck above. She slips into the shadows with me. Maybe Kammi told her where I was, or maybe she just knew, like she knows about other things.

"Your mother, she is very upset."

I shrug.

"Is no right, you and she."

I still don't say anything.

Martia mutters to herself in Papiamentu. Then she starts again in English. "Tomorrow is the party at the Bindases'."

"Does Mother want to cancel?" She can't. I have to confront Mayur, to see what he thinks he knows.

"No, no, is important to go. The Bindases are big people here. Some are with the government."

Yes, Dr. Bindas is associated with the hospital in Willemstad, and his cousin is supposed to be in government. Mother never mentions the connection, though Mayur brags about it when he can. Mother will want people to think there is nothing wrong, so she won't cancel, even if she doesn't want to go.

Martia sighs and smiles. She holds her hand out as if I am a small child who's threatened to run away and she wants to pack a lunch for me so that after I find a hiding place down the block, I'll eat my lunch and go back home. Home, where they're supposed to love you and want you back.

"Everybody today is in bad mood," she says. "It's time to *kome*, to eat. Come now."

I'd say I'm not hungry, but Martia would know that I'm lying.

CHAPTER FIFTEEN

AT FIVE the next afternoon, Mother, Kammi, and I follow the shell road to the Bindases' house. Before Mother can fix her everything-is-fine face, Mrs. Bindas waves us onto the beach from the edge of the green lawn. She smiles, her head tilted at an angle, as if she's seen a family argument she's not meant to witness.

Only we aren't saying anything out loud.

We're a silent trio. We've been that way for a whole day, since the plein air trip, since Kammi asked Mother about the blue boat. We are three corners of a triangle, sharp-angled and equidistant.

Mother steps first onto the sand, shakes off her slides. Kammi follows, picking up her shoes and tapping the heels together gently just like Mother. I wonder if she knows she's mirroring Mother or whether it's just instinct. She already seems to have fallen into the rhythm of living here.

"Come, we have soft drinks. Coco Rico, Fria. Ice cold." Mrs. Bindas leads us to a tent sheltering coolers of drinks. Beer in one cooler and bright orange and green bottles of sodas in another.

Down the beach, away from the bonfire and the tents, six boys throw Frisbees to each other in a relay. One of them, the short one, stops when he turns around and looks our way, heads toward us.

Mayur.

Mrs. Bindas beams. "Mayur, see your special guests, they have come. You should bring your cousins over, introduce them to the American girls."

"They're busy. Come on, I'll take you to them," Mayur says to us, and turns to walk back down the beach. He assumes we'll follow. On command, Kammi does. I grab a glass bottle of Coco Rico, my favorite coconut-flavored soda, from the ice. A servant—not the boy from our first visit—opens it for me, tossing the metal cap into a basket behind him without looking. Ignoring me, except I see his gaze slide over my chest. He steps past to rearrange the ice around the bottles in the cooler.

Mrs. Bindas and Mother wander over to a cluster of beach chairs where other women sit drinking, their scarves and skirts fluttering like birds around them. The men gather around another fire, their laughter but not their words carrying between the crashes of the surf.

Yards behind, I trail Mayur and Kammi.

When I catch up, Mayur has gathered all the other boys around. His cousins from Trinidad. Some other boys, too; locals. Not so rich, I can see it in their eyes. Several don't usually get a whole soda for themselves. They stand in a semicircle, looking at their bare feet, taking chugs from soda bottles they've planted in the sand. They won't look directly at Kammi. Because she's a girl, because she's American, because she's pretty. One boy looks up when I kick sand over his foot; then his gaze skims over Kammi before he looks away again. He's thin and rangy, like the other boys, except for Mayur. Dark-skinned, too, with brown eyes that seem to miss little.

"This is Roberto, Tibor, and Saco. They're my cousins. Some others are over there." He points to the men around the far bonfire. "And the others here, Loco, Alonzo, and Klaus."

"Cyan says you're from Trinidad," Kammi says to Roberto. "What's that like?"

The boys shrug, then grin, still looking at their feet or out to sea. How to explain the difference? Another island in the same sea.

"Do you want to play?" Mayur asks. His mother probably bribed him to say that. I look over my shoulder, see Mrs. Bindas wave. Mother has her back to us, her hand holding a glass of wine in the air, perfectly balanced. Posed. Mayur doesn't return his mother's wave.

Despite herself, Kammi looks at me.

"No thanks," I answer. "I'll watch." I hate running after the Frisbee when the wind grabs it from my reach. I hate missing it, chasing it as it rolls zigzagging down the slope toward the surf.

Mayur holds out the Frisbee to Kammi. "You go first." He's playing host. This is his party, after all. He's the big man. The other boys know it, too.

Kammi takes the Frisbee. "Thanks. I used to play this with my Dad's black Labrador. Have you ever seen dogs that can jump and catch them midair?"

Some of the boys nod. Saco grins, his black hair flopping over his eyes. His is the kind of face most girls like. Soft and cute, his eyes are those of a black Lab.

"*Claro*, we've seen that," Mayur says, shrugging, acting bored. "I had a dog once, he was a champion Frisbee catcher." Sure he did.

I squat in the sand, spread my skirt around myself like a picnic blanket. Howard has a dog? Mother has never mentioned that. Neither has Howard, and he's never brought one around in Maine. Mother doesn't even like dogs. I wonder where it is now. Maybe in Atlanta with Kammi's mother. I can hear Howard saying it. "Kammi needs a dog. With the breakup, this is just the thing. I'll miss Old Pete or whatever his name is, but it's for Kammi. Nothing's too good for Kammi." Howard doesn't really talk that way—his voice is way too business-school to sound so breathless—but I can imagine him almost saying it like that. Getting rid of the dog and making it sound like he's doing it for Kammi, when he's really doing it for Mother. Has Kammi's mother figured that out?

The disc thuds at my side, spewing sand onto my skirt. I squint into the sun. "Hey, watch it."

I fling the Frisbee away, and the wind picks it up, arcs it toward the sun and down, straight for Mayur. Figures.

The boy closest to me, I think it's Loco, laughs. He thinks I meant to aim for Mayur. I shake my head.

The relay continues. Every two times around the circle of boys, one of them shoots the Frisbee straight for Kammi. She catches it and passes it to her right, in a straight line, from the hip. Straight to Saco, who doesn't seem to notice he's the favored one. He slams the Frisbee on to another boy, hard enough that it makes a whizzing sound.

The sun edges down the sky. Unlike Maine, where the light lingers past dusk, even in the winter, here the sun is out and then it's just gone, as if someone pulls down a shade at the end of the day.

When it's dark, the servants stoke the fires. Three bonfires line the beach like search flares, just like the night they found Dad. I stare into the flames and watch the embers catch the breeze and float heavenward.

The servants roast hot dogs and sausages on one of the bonfires. Mrs. Bindas waves us to the tent with the food.

"Such an American custom," she says. "We thought you'd like it. Hot dogs and potato crisps, just like your Fourth of July, Independence Day, yes?" Mrs. Bindas asks as we all collect plates and napkins and move through the line. She says crisps instead of chips. Plates full, Kammi and I follow the boys to their fire, leaving the adults to gather around their own.

Kammi sits beside me on a driftwood log the boys dragged up from the beach. She acts unsure, as if she may not want to. She presses her knees together and sits tall.

The boys devour their hot dogs. They run crusts of buns along the rims of the plates, scooping up any mustard or hot dog juice. They go back for seconds. Kammi holds her bun in both hands, careful not to let the hot dog slip out or the mustard run down her fingers. One of the older boys, Klaus, throws a chip at Mayur, who ducks and tosses an empty soda bottle back. Mayur misses, but Klaus doesn't even flinch.

"Have you been to Mount Christoffel?" Kammi asks Saco.

Mayur is the one who answers. "Yes," he says, and shrugs. "When the cousins come, we always hike there. Don't we?" The other boys all nod, looking at each other.

"Is it very high?"

"No, not so high." He looks at Kammi, her feet planted close together in the sand. "If you're used to hiking."

Ha. Mayur talks about hiking like he talks about swimming. Kammi one-upped him last time, about the swim team, but this time she doesn't take him on. Maybe she thinks that since the boys outnumber her, Mayur won't be so easy to defeat. Or maybe she doesn't want to insult Saco.

Mrs. Bindas makes her way over, carrying a basket of marshmallows. She hands it to Mayur, along with a trash bag for our used plates, and gives him thin sticks to use for roasting. "Another American custom. We thought this might be fun."

After his mother leaves, Mayur rips open the bag of marshmallows. He shows the other boys how to skewer them and toast the edges, pulling them out of the flames just before they catch fire. The gooey sweetness, just shy of burned, tastes delicious. He gives the first sample to Kammi, who giggles as she takes it. When she can't get the stickiness off her fingers, she licks them clean.

Loco finishes next, and he passes his stick to me. I frown. "Thanks." I pull off the marshmallow, even though it's hot, and pop it into my mouth. I give the boy back his stick without looking at him, and he threads two more marshmallows on as if he's baiting a hook.

The other boys jostle for room to toast their own marshmallows. Mayur scoots close to Kammi and me.

Kammi jumps up. "I'm going for another soda," she says. "Want one?"

"Sure. Okay. A Coco," I say.

"Mayur?" she asks. Always polite.

"No."

"I'll help you," Saco says, propping his marshmallow stick against the log.

Mayur turns his head and watches Kammi and Saco walk away.

"I know," he says.

"Know what?"

"About your father."

"You said that before. What do you mean?" Mayur doesn't know what happened. The police don't know. No one knows. Maybe Dad didn't even realize what was happening to him.

"It was in the report."

Now I know he's lying. Nothing was in the report. At least, not the report that Mother and I were given.

"There wasn't anything in the report." Except that he died by drowning.

"Maybe you don't believe me." Mayur yanks his marshmallow out of the fire, blows out the flames.

"Why should I?"

"My cousin, he works in investigations. He's very important."

"No one knew Dr. Bindas at the commissioner's office."

Mayur looks at me sharply. So he didn't think I'd actually try to find out on my own. "His name isn't Bindas. I just said he was a cousin."

"So, tell me." Mayur would say his cousin was important even if he were just the janitor in the police station. But what if he does know something? And, if so, why wasn't it reported to Mother? Why wasn't it in the newspapers?

"If you want me to tell you, you better be nice to me." Mayur holds out the marshmallow, roasted to perfection, tempting me to take it. And I do.

CHAPTER SIXTEEN

I START TO ask him why I should be nice, why he should tell me at all. I think he's lying. Mayur just likes to be important.

"Hey, what are you talking about?" Loco plops down on the sand in front of Mayur and me. He throws a bottle cap into the fire. He holds a new bottle of soda loosely by the neck. He runs his hand over the lip, as if to brush away sand or salt, then guzzles from it. He burps, long and loud.

Mayur laughs. No, he howls, the way boys do. Some of the cousins laugh, too, punching each other's shoulders, as if this is the funniest thing they've ever heard. Even the taller ones, the older ones, act like little boys. They're laughing so hard, they act as if they've forgotten what Mayur was talking about, why Loco even asked what was going on.

Kammi and Saco wander back into the circle of light around the bonfire. Kammi sits on the log next to me, but farther away than before. Saco sits near her.

I shuffle my bare feet in the sand, burying them in the coolness.

The moment when I could ask Mayur what he means has passed for now.

Mayur speaks into my ear as he pushes his pudgy body off the sand. "Remember, be nice, and I'll tell you," he says, seeming to read my mind. "Later."

"Do you swim at night?" Loco asks. He's looking at Kammi and me.

"Isn't that dangerous?" Kammi straightens her back as she sits forward on the log, no doubt thinking about how dark the sea is at night. What things could brush against a leg, or take it off?

Loco shrugs. "What is dangerous? Not *peligroso*. Not here, no sharks."

"It's okay. It's shallow just here." Saco sounds reassuring.

Sharks feed in shallow waters at dusk and dawn. That much I remember from the nature shows Dad encouraged me to watch all the time.

"Okay, who's in?" Mayur asks.

The boys speak all at once.

"For a minute. I'll go in for a minute," Kammi says when Saco grins at her.

"What about you?" Loco asks me.

"I don't swim in the ocean." I pull my scarf around my shoulders.

"This is just a sea, like a bathtub." Saco grins, his eyes lit up by the glow from the fire. Kammi's watching him. She'll go in the water if he wants her to.

I shake my head.

Mayur narrows his eyes at me. "She's afraid."

He thinks he can dare me to go in. His words don't scare me. I don't care if they all think I am a coward. At the end of the month, I'll go back to Maine. I won't have to see them again. Next summer, I'll find a way to stay with Zoe while Mother comes back here. Maybe she won't even bring Howard, since she told Philippa on the phone last year that bringing men here is bad luck. Kammi won't come, either; she'll spend time with her mother in Atlanta or have "quality" time with Howard. I can see it now. Like the points of a triangle, we'll stay in our separate corners.

"She doesn't have to come in," Loco says. "She can watch from the beach, yell if she sees a shark."

As if I could see a fin in the dark water, even with the waxing moon and the phosphorescence on the waves. But Loco is trying to be nice. For a boy.

The boys, including Saco, whoop and race each other to the water. Kammi unties her skirt, steps out of it, and folds it, revealing her pink bikini underneath. She looks toward Mother and Mrs. Bindas. To see if they're watching the boys run into the surf. To see if they raise a warning flag. They're

too busy laughing around their own fire. The men aren't looking our way, either.

"Saco said Mayur knows something about your father,"
Kammi says, still not looking at me. She pulls her linen
blouse over her head, folds it carefully, just like her skirt.

I close my eyes.

"Do you think he really knows?" she asks.

I shrug.

"Do you care?" Kammi's voice hardens.

I open my eyes. "I do. But why would *you*?"

Kammi steps backwards. She turns and races to the black
water tinged with silver, as if she'll dive in and swoop it up
into her arms. At least it will be welcoming, even if it's dangerous.

I follow them to the shore and watch, letting the surf
glide over my bare feet. I seek sea glass with my toes, but
everything feels like grains of sand or bits of shell. There's no
point in dredging up sand and running it through my fingers
in the darkness. After a storm, after the tides come in full
and go out, and the sun rises, that's the best time to look for
sea glass.

The boys yell and dive and show off. Two even do hand-
stands. Only their legs stick up out of the water. I imagine
their faces pressed against the sandy bottom, how they hold
their breath and how their eyes bulge when their lungs crave
air and they spring to the surface, gasping.

Shouts come from behind me. A couple of men, one of

them Dr. Bindas, dash into the waves, demanding that everybody get out of the water. "Out, come on out!"

Mother, breathless, appears at my side. She grabs my arm. "Where's Kammi?"

"There." I point. Kammi is closest to shore. She's waving her arms, sweeping water over her head. She turns at the shouts.

Mother drops her hand from my arm. "Why didn't you stop her?"

"Everyone went in." Everyone but me. "Mayur says it's safe."

"So if everyone jumps off a cliff, that's your excuse? Someone says it's safe?" Mother's voice rises. "Kammi's our guest. What if something happens to her?" Like it did to Dad, she means. But she doesn't say it out loud.

I do. "Like drowning?"

Mother sets her mouth in her tight, flat way. "Whose fault would that be?" She steps past me to meet Kammi, motioning her forward. "Kammi, come on. Aren't you cold?"

Kammi splashes out, the sea coursing down her skin. She's laughing, just like the boys. Not even Dr. Bindas's scolding makes them sheepish.

Mrs. Bindas bustles to the water's edge, a stack of towels under each arm. She makes each boy take one, though they try to scoot out of her reach. Mother takes one for Kammi, wraps her into it against the breeze. Kammi's teeth chatter, but she's grinning, I see as we get closer to the bonfire.

"We're going home. Right now," Mother says. "Get Kammi's things."

I grab Kammi's neat stack of dry clothes off the log.

"I'm okay, Mrs. Walters. That was fun. I've never been in the sea at night." Kammi picks up her shoes, holds them in the hand not holding the towel around her. "Mrs. Bindas, thank you for the party."

Kammi's beaming. Saco comes close. He sweeps his hair back from his face, water still streaming down his neck. He smiles.

"Good night," he says.

Kammi says good night back.

Mother steps between them. "We'll send Martia back tomorrow with this towel," she says to Mrs. Bindas. "Thank you." She keeps watching Saco leave while telling Mrs. Bindas about how delightful everything was, how much like an American party it all turned out to be.

Mrs. Bindas clucks over Kammi's wet hair.

"She must go home, get dry. Children, always they are not thinking." Mrs. Bindas is clucking at Mayur, too, but not in anger. She's more like a hen hovering over a chick that's been out in the rain. Like Martia would do.

Mother is already stalking toward the lawn, to wipe the sand from her feet. She'll put her shoes back on to protect her feet against broken shells on the walk back.

CHAPTER SEVENTEEN

ON SUNDAY MORNING, Martia rises even earlier than usual so she can make breakfast before she walks down the road to catch the bus for her home near Santa Rosa. I can hear her in the kitchen. Once, when I was little, I ran after her as she left. I wanted to go with her. Martia might have let me, and Mother might have relented, but Dad said no, Martia needed her day off from *Blauwe Huis*—and all its inhabitants. Even me. Having Martia leave made her return all the better, even when she didn't bring me any sweets. Once, she brought me a picture of a stick house she said her little boy had drawn on the rough brown paper I'd sent home with her, the paper Mother said was good enough for me to use for drawing. In the yard, he'd drawn chickens with three-toed feet twice the size of their bodies.

I wait until I hear Martia turn the key in the front door before I slip into the kitchen. On the counter, she's left fresh-chopped fruit and fresh-squeezed orange juice, with a basket of mango-filled pastries under a yellow linen towel. I have some juice and make up a tray to take back to my room. On the way back, I remove the master bedroom key from the hook by the locked cabinet where Martia stores her herbs and spices, and probably healing potions she keeps for emergencies. When I was young, I was sure Martia stored powerful remedies that in the wrong hands could be poisonous. I slip the key into my pocket for later, when I'll look in the room.

When I get back to my room, the door is open, and Kammi perches on the edge of my unmade bed. She holds my hinged box of sea glass in her lap. The orange juice sours in my stomach. She jerks when I enter the room.

"You had more of this glass before," she says, as if she's going to ask a question about what I did with the rest of it. "You should do something with it." She holds up a handful of glass pieces.

"Do something?" I slide the tray of fruit and pastries onto my dresser and take the box from her. I snap the lid shut on the sea glass. The box feels cool in my hands.

"Yes, you could turn it into jewelry. I've seen some girls do that with beads and glass. They wrap wire around it, make bracelets. You shouldn't just leave it in a box."

Kammi's being nice, even now, and I don't want her to be.

"Don't tell me what to do." I squeeze the closed lid as if it's Pandora's box.

Tears well in her eyes. She's probably thinking this is the month from hell and when is it going to end? Instead of running away or crying, though, she nods and crosses her arms, holding her hands against her sides, protecting herself.

"What are we going to do today?" she asks.

We?

"This is Martia's day off. She already plugged in Mother's coffee and set the timer for eight. That's when Mother will come down, not a minute before," I say, restoring the box to the top of the dresser. It's now two hours before Mother is likely to come downstairs.

Kammi nods, as if I've told her a big secret.

"After last night, you should stay out of her way," I say, raising my eyebrows toward the studio above us.

"Why?" Kammi's face turns up, too, as if there's a clue written on the ceiling.

"You know, the water. Saco following you around like a puppy."

Kammi blushes, the pink undertones blossoming on her cheeks. "He wasn't following me."

"Right, Kammi. You're supposed to be the artist, the observant one. Mother said so. You should be able to tell what a boy is up to."

"How about Loco?" she asks shyly, but with the corners

of her mouth upturned. Because of Saco or because Mother said she was an artist, I can't tell.

"A boy named Crazy. What do you think?"

"It's just a name. He seemed very nice."

"Compared to Mayur, who wouldn't be?"

Kammi scoots over to let me sit on the bed with her. "What should we do?"

"We" again. "We could go back to the Bindases' and ask to swim in the pool. Mrs. Bindas gave us a standing offer. I'm sure Saco is still there." That might alarm Mother, which alone would make the trip worth it. More important, though, is what Mayur said. Maybe Saco would tell Kammi if he knows. For Kammi, he might even ask the right questions, get Mayur to give up his secret.

Even though she grins, Kammi shakes her head. "Something else."

"Ostrich farm?" I say.

Kammi shivers. "Not again."

"Hato Cave?"

"Are there bats?"

"The bats only fly at night." At dusk, they swoop out of the cave to hunt. By day, they hang from the ceiling, their guano mounding up on the floor. The cave is cool, I remember, and damp. Mother stayed outside while Dad and I took the tour. The only thing I hated was when the guide took us into one chamber and turned off the lights. Dad held my hand.

"I don't think so." Kammi shakes her head. "Not today."

I hold up the key.

"What's that for?" Kammi's nose wrinkles, the funny way it does when she thinks something is off.

"The master bedroom."

"Why is it locked?"

"Why do you think?"

Kammi stares at the key as if it holds a secret. "It was your parents' room. Last summer."

"An A for you. Come on," I say. "We have time now. Before Mother gets up. We can only go there on Martia's day off. She misses nothing." If she found us, she'd shoo us out to the beach. To get out in the sun—"Remember the sun screening," she would say. Blue curaçao, blue heaven. We shouldn't be locked away in the house when paradise waits outside.

The doorknob is shiny brass, almost freshly polished, with no fingerprints smudging the golden surface. My face reflected in the handle looks misshapen, as if I'm some circus freak.

I turn the key, and the latch clicks. I twist the handle and push, careful not to let the door bang against the back wall—it sometimes did last summer when Dad forgot that the hinges had been greased. The room seems the same, just musty, like any room unopened for a long time. When I close the door behind Kammi, I turn the handle carefully so that it doesn't click, even though Martia's not here. She can hear me from the kitchen crinkling a candy wrapper in my room in the hour before *cena*. "*Basta*, child," she'll say. "Enough. There will be good food for dinner, wait." But she doesn't really mean it, since she shakes her head and lets me finish what I'm eating anyway, hiding the wrapper inside a paper napkin before tossing it in the trash. In case Mother checks. We are allies.

Slivers of light filter through the closed window shades. Bright lines cut across the wooden floor. Palm-tree linens cover the bed. The puffy pillows—the kind Mother likes—are plumped, just waiting to cradle a head.

I nod at Kammi, who tiptoes over and creaks open drawers in the bedside table. I check the tall dresser. I peek into the dark spaces behind the drawers, looking for a corner of torn paper that's gotten stuck. But there are no letters tucked away, no forgotten receipts. Everything's clean.

As she stands over an open drawer, Kammi whispers, "What are you looking for?"

"Anything interesting." I want to say "clues" but I'm not sure she'd understand. She doesn't know everything. She doesn't know that my mother might have known Howard when my Dad was still alive. That might be a clue.

The wind starts to slap the window and the branches outside, zigzagging the morning light across the floor. With sunrise, the island heats, and the breezes start to blow landward again.

"It's time," I say.

I turn the handle as carefully as when we entered the

room. I peek to make sure the hallway is empty. Kammi goes first, tiptoeing back to her room. As soon as she's safely inside, I tug the door closed behind me. In the stillness, the click sounds loud.

In my room I fall onto the bed and stretch out. A successful foray, even though nothing turned up. I finish breakfast, then bus my tray back to the kitchen, this time slapping my flip-flops along the floor, making as much noise as I can. Before I empty the dishes into the sink—Martia always says to leave them for her—I replace the key on its hook.

As I'm leaving the room, the coffeepot gurgles into action, and a bitter aroma seeps into the air.

CHAPTER EIGHTEEN

K AMMI AND I escape the house before Mother comes downstairs for her coffee. After Kammi takes a quick dip in the sea, we find shady spots on the upper deck, just off the living room. Kammi scoots her art bin next to her lounge chair, as if she believes she might learn how to paint by instinct, just by being close to the tools of the trade. She runs her hands over the smooth wooden handles of the paintbrushes. I imagine the tickle of the coarse bristles over the tender inside of her arm.

I hold Kammi's horse series paperback, the spine now hopelessly bent, in front of me. It's so boring I can't make myself read the second chapter. Instead, I squint over the top of the page. In the distance, the sea seems to bend along the horizon and the sky pivots to counterbalance. Near the shoreline, the water is pure turquoise. I wonder which colored pencils in the back of my closet at home I would have to blend to match the exact hue.

The French doors open. Mother holds a coffee cup in one hand and closes the door with the other, a newspaper tucked under her arm. It's the local paper, I can tell from the banner. The articles are written in Dutch or English, sometimes Spanish, and even Papiamentu, as if whoever writes the article decides which language best suits the particular story. I imagine an article about the trade deficit in formal Dutch, reviews about the best shops on the cruise-ship circuit in English, a crime report in Papiamentu.

"You're both up early." Mother says it as if she doesn't trust us together in Martia's absence. Maybe she thinks we sneaked out last night and went back to the Bindases' beach party, swimming until dawn. Kammi's hair is damp from her morning dip. Mother's gaze takes in that fact.

I think Kammi misses the look. She's already staring down at her lap, her face beginning to turn pink. Maybe she thinks Mother can read guilt in her face about the master bedroom—for no reason, as we found nothing. Or guilt about being friendly to me, who let her swim at night at the Bindases' house in the first place, when she's here to make Mother her ally and to learn how to paint to make Howard happy.

"Dad always said the early bird catches the worm," I say.

Mother sits down under the umbrella chair. Her coffee sloshes over the brim of her cup.

Kammi jumps up and wipes the arm of Mother's chair with her beach towel.

"Thank you, Kammi." Mother picks up her saucer so Kammi can wipe underneath.

"You're welcome." Kammi shifts her weight from foot to foot, still holding the coffee-stained towel.

"Just go rinse that in cold water, save Martia having to bleach that stain." Mother dismisses Kammi. Mother has never said anything before about how to reduce Martia's workload.

Kammi scrambles into the house.

"About last night," Mother says, slapping the folded newspaper onto the table.

I raise the book back to eye level and try to focus on reading each word, seeing each individual letter.

Kammi comes running. "Mrs. Bindas is at the door. I'll go let her in." She disappears again before Mother can say anything. Did Saco or Mayur come with Mrs. Bindas?

"Why is she here?" Mother mutters to herself.

"Maybe for your saltwater taffy recipe. I told her how everyone brings back saltwater taffy from their beach vacations. But homemade is best." I'm lying, but Mother can't tell for sure. After all, Mrs. Bindas did say she wanted the party to be like an American Fourth of July, though it was only June, still June.

Kammi escorts Mrs. Bindas to the deck.

"Please don't disturb," Mrs. Bindas says, waving Mother

back into her chair. Mother had hardly moved. "I am early, but I couldn't wait."

"I'll bring you some tea," Kammi says.

Mrs. Bindas watches Kammi dash away again. "Such a lovely girl. It is happiness, such a girl." Her eyes linger on the doorway.

A stiff smile settles itself on Mother's face. So practiced.

"Thank you again for the cookout," Mother says. "The girls—and I—had a wonderful time."

"Especially at the end. Kammi loved the night swim," I say. Mother's smile falters.

Mrs. Bindas doesn't stop beaming. "We are being so happy. Very sorry, though, for Mayur about the swimming. There was no cause to worry us all. Boys, you know." I try to imagine Mayur being sorry for anything.

Kammi eases the French door open with her foot. She's chosen to serve tea in the Dutch owner's expensive china, the set that's stored behind glass-door cabinets. It's nicer than the everyday set Mother's using. The bright cup, the color of yellow-winged parrots, reminds me of Mrs. Bindas herself, the way the folds of her sari drape like layered bird feathers.

Mrs. Bindas claps her hands together, then presses them to her cheeks, as if to cool them, as if Kammi has overwhelmed her. "What beautiful china. Truly Dutch, antique. I've seen the pattern in collectors' catalogs. Thank you, my dear."

Kammi grins and settles herself on the deck chair, turning it to be part of the circle.

With miniature silver tongs, Mrs. Bindas grasps sugar cubes one at a time, dropping a total of three into her cup, and adds a splash of cream. She stirs with the tiny spoon Kammi tucked on the saucer. The art of arrangement: Kammi has the gift, too, like Mother. But Kammi's seems real. Not practiced.

How can Kammi be so open when she is the stranger here?

"You must be very tired, from hosting the cookout." Mother hints that Mrs. Bindas shouldn't stay long.

"The servants, they do most of the work. Having friends and family visit, it is no chore." Mrs. Bindas sips tea, her bejeweled fingers glimmering in the morning sun that's crept onto the deck, chasing the shade away. Soon, the only shadows will be underneath the deck.

Mother slips her sunglasses from atop her head onto her nose. Shields in place, like some force field in a science fiction movie. Waiting to hear why Mrs. Bindas has come.

I squint at the sea again, watching the sparkling water, the play of light over color.

"Last night, after the girls left, Mayur and his cousins, they had the best idea." Mrs. Bindas sips more tea. So here comes the reason for her visit.

Mother presses her sunglasses against the bridge of her nose. Maybe she's getting another headache.

Kammi nudges my foot. She grins when I look her way. I betray nothing. No reaction for Mother to study. But I am curious. Maybe there is a way to find out more from Mayur. "The boys are going to hike Mount Christoffel. Next Saturday morning, very early. While the air is still cool. They suggested inviting Cyan and Kammi. Dr. Bindas and I think this is a splendid idea."

"A hike?" On the surface, Mother's voice gives nothing away, but I hear her undertone of disapproval.

"Oh, the girls, they will be very safe." Mrs. Bindas places her cup and saucer on the table delicately. "Dr. Bindas, he will go along. They'll take a, how do you say? A picnic lunch."

"A picnic? Oh, that's sounds fun," Kammi says, looking at Mother, probably trying to read her behind her glasses.

"Not too rigorous?" Mother asks.

Mrs. Bindas titters. "No, of course not. They will park at the closest place to hike up. Only two hours. Mayur would not ask the girls on a too-hard hike." Mrs. Bindas doesn't say anything more about the beach party, about the boys going into the surf at night and Kammi following them in. Or about the adults' reaction.

"Who's going?"

"Mayur, of course. His cousins Saco and Roberto. And his friend Loco. They were all at the cookout."

When Mrs. Bindas says Saco's name, Kammi smiles. At Loco's name, she looks at me from under her lashes.

Mother frowns. "Any girls?"

Mrs. Bindas shakes her head. "Only boys in our family." She spreads her arms, her bangle bracelets tinkling together like glass wind chimes. She shrugs. "What are we to do?"

"It'll be hot."

"Oh, that is no worry. The boys will carry plenty of cold water. And Dr. Bindas, he is a medical doctor, you know." Mrs. Bindas smiles, as if being a doctor is the answer to every problem. Mrs. Bindas doesn't betray whether she re-members that Dr. Bindas met the boat when they brought my father in from the sea. He did not bring Dad back to life. He only confirmed that Dad was dead before the officials drove his body off to the morgue.

Mother finally looks toward Kammi. "You're sure you want to go?"

"Yes," Kammi says, looking at me.

"Cyan?" Mother asks.

"I'll go." I've never been to the top of Mount Christoffel. By the time I was old enough to hike it, Dad had stopped coming with us, spending his Junes in Italy or somewhere with his language students or on a research trip instead. Last summer, when he finally came with us again, he and I planned to hike the mountain the last weekend in June.

"Mayur will be so pleased," Mrs. Bindas says.

Pleased he can show off.

"Also, I am so hoping that before you leave us this year,

you will honor us. Dr. Bindas and I say for shame we have had no exhibition of your artwork."

Mother shakes her head. "You are very kind. But I come here to paint. And relax."

Mrs. Bindas's smile droops, then revives. "You are too modest. Yes, it is decided. We will host a reception—that is what you call it, yes?—for your artwork. Before you leave."

Mother stands. "Really, that's impossible. My paintings are in galleries in New York. In Atlanta. Nothing I have here is suitable." She doesn't admit that there are no paintings here, except the untouched canvases upstairs.

"I'm sure you could have something ready by then," I say, knowing the canvases stand empty.

Mother's eyes flash at me. "Don't be silly." She faces Mrs. Bindas, who has risen. "I'm sure you understand. An exhibition takes a lot of lead time. All those paintings to wrap and ship. It would take months to get ready. My agent would have to be consulted. The insurance." She explains as if there would never be enough time to prepare for an exhibition here in Curaçao.

Mrs. Bindas straightens her sari. Her smile does not fade. "Of course, it is too much to ask. But perhaps a small reception, just a few friends of mine. Influential women who are liking art. They dabble a little, too. Maybe we each bring a single painting from this summer. It would be enough, yes?"

"I—I'll have to see." Mother concedes this much, at least, enough to keep Mrs. Bindas happy. Mother will hate reviewing the amateur works of Mrs. Bindas's friends. But it might be better than a reception in her honor alone.

"Excellent. Girls," Mrs. Bindas says, turning to Kammi and me. "Next Saturday, we will pick you up. Seven o'clock in the morning."

"Seven?" Mother asks.

Mrs. Bindas shakes her head as she starts toward the door. "I know. So early. But best to hike before the heat. No one to have sunstroke, Dr. Bindas says. We'll stop for breakfast on the way. A café near Savonet."

"Thank you, Mrs. Bindas," Kammi says.

"And always, of course, you are welcome to swim at our pool. Always welcome."

I follow Mrs. Bindas and Kammi to the door, as much to avoid being on the deck alone with Mother as to say goodbye to Mrs. Bindas.

CHAPTER NINETEEN

MARTIA NO LONGER says anything when I leave the house at first light to look for sea glass. No words of warning about undertow—she knows I won't go into the water. Nothing about the wild donkeys that sometimes wander through, munching prized vegetation. Instead, without speaking, she leaves a guava pastry on a waxed-paper square and a water bottle on the counter for me. I've devoured the pastry by the time I reach the waterline.

This morning the sea is glass itself, like a green bottle, and the surf overnight has yielded few treasures. Some broken shells, a washed-up jellyfish. I don't even find any prized blues near the outwash. The boring brown pieces seem too sharp, too raw, like beer bottles recently tossed overboard from some party boat or washed down from the hills. I leave them to the sea, to have their edges ground smooth.

When I reach the point, I hike my way to the top of the small rise. I sit on a piece of driftwood that someone's dragged this far and left as the perfect seat from which to watch the morning sea.

June 21 already. Mother and I haven't talked about the coming date. Today may be the longest span of daylight of the year, the summer solstice, but in two days it will be June 23 again, the longest day of my life. As sure as the earth turns on its axis, the seasons change. There's a time to mourn, and a time to turn from mourning. Is this what we are doing—Mother and I—in our own ways, like magnets pushing each other away? On the twenty-third, after a whole year has passed, are we supposed to stop? Turn everything off, all our feelings, and let Howard move into the Maine house? Adopt Kammi as our own and set up her easel and paints near a window with a southern exposure?

A group of boys jog along the beach, splashing through the surf, kicking up wet sand. Laughing, they pass close in front of me, but they don't turn to look. They'd recognize me if they did. I know them. Saco's running in front. Panting, Mayur brings up the rear. How will he ever hike Mount Christoffel on Saturday?

The boys stop before they get close to our house, before they've crossed an imaginary property line. They look toward it, and then they wave in unison at someone standing on the deck. I squint. It wouldn't be Mother. She'd be in her studio near the widow's walk, higher still, except that it's not even eight o'clock yet. Martia, maybe? She might be sweeping the sand off the deck, careful not to drag the furniture for fear of disturbing Mother, who demands quiet in the mornings.

The figure comes down from the deck and meets the boys on the beach. They crowd around.

By the time I get there, Kammi's at the center of the group of boys.

"Where'd you go?" she asks when she sees me. The boys part around her like a river around a rock.

"I walk the beach every morning."

"What's in the bag?" Mayur asks.

Before I answer, Loco elbows his way between Mayur and me. "If you want shells," Loco says, "we know a good spot. Where they aren't broken up. Off the reef." He's pointing up the beach, on the other side of *Blauwe Huis*. "You have to swim out past it."

"It's safe," Saco says to Kammi.

Kammi looks from Saco to me.

"I'm not looking for shells," I say, gripping the plastic bag harder in my fist even though it's empty, as if someone might take it and look inside.

"I like to pick up shells," Kammi says. "At Sanibel Island, in Florida, the beaches have thousands of shells. So many you can't walk barefoot."

Saco nods, serious. "I know a beach like that here, too. It's on the other side of the island. Maybe we can go—"

"Hello." A voice carries on the wind. Mother waves from the widow's walk. Up early. Maybe she heard the voices after all and decided she'd better worry about Kammi. Because she can't trust all those boys, and she can't trust me to protect Kammi. Not after the nighttime swim at the Bindases' house.

Saco hesitates, but then he waves, and the other boys do, too. He's the leader. Even though Mayur thinks he is, because it's his beach and his house and his father's a doctor.

"Come over for breakfast. Martia, we have company." Mother goes back inside, but I can still hear her calling for Martia. When Mrs. Bindas came to visit, Mother couldn't wait for her to leave. Now Mother's asking for the boys to come closer. She wants to meet them, check them out herself before she lets Kammi go hiking with them.

Saco opens his mouth, but Mother's already disappeared.

"Mother wants to meet you before the hike," I say.

Mayur says, "She was at the cookout."

"That was before the hiking invitation. She wants to make sure no one's going to push Kammi off a cliff," I say.

"That's not true," Kammi says, blushing.

"Okay, so maybe no one's going to push *you* off a cliff," I say.

Martia appears on the deck. She's carrying a tray. "Breakfast," she calls.

Mayur barrels his way forward, the other boys following his lead. Saco waits with Kammi and me. Funny how when other people are around, Mayur assumes his princely role. Kammi is *his* guest for the hike, so he goes first in the natural order of things.

Martia has filled a blue and white tray with pastries and rolls, butter and jam. We walk onto the deck, where the boys stand around in a circle, their backs against the railing. A moment later, Martia returns with a pitcher of chilled passion-fruit juice and thin plastic cups that, when empty, will blow away in the wind. She fills the cups and passes them around.

Mother appears, putting herself into the circle of boys. "I didn't have a chance to meet most of you at the cookout." She hasn't asked a question of them yet, so they don't say anything.

Then Mayur steps forward. "These are my cousins, Saco and Roberto. This is Loco—his real name is Achal." Mayur introduces the other boys, too.

Mother smiles at each in turn, studying them. "Ah, yes, Saco, I've heard of you." She says it as a warning, though she sounds like she's teasing.

Too late, Kammi steps away from him, already having drawn enemy fire to him by standing too close.

Loco refills his own cup, as if he isn't a guest. "Mayur's mother says you are an artist. What do you paint?"

Mother folds her arms. "Landscapes, still lifes."

"Like fruit bowls and bottles?" Loco asks.

Mayur laughs and punches his cousin in the shoulder. Mother blanches. Loco doesn't seem to realize he's insulted her. Maybe he really is crazy. Or maybe he's truly interested.

"It's not just junk on a table," I answer. I'm not defending Mother but I don't want her to say something rude to Loco, even though he doesn't mean anything to me. "Still lifes are carefully composed. It's all about balancing shapes and colors."

"Like Cézanne? The way he drapes the folds of cloth next to the fruit?"

"Yes." Maybe Loco's not so crazy.

"We have to go," Mayur says, making a display of handing his cup back to Martia so it won't blow away and litter the beach. "Mother's driver is taking us into Willemstad to the arcade." He doesn't ask if we can go. He's just showing off. "Thank you, Mrs. Walters. Don't forget Saturday." As he walks by me, he says low, so only I hear, "Maybe I have something for you. On Saturday."

"So tell," I whisper.

"If you're nice."

"Thank you," Saco says to Mother and Martia as he turns away stiffly. He knows Mother doesn't approve of him, just because he appears to like Kammi. Loco and the other boys mumble thanks, too, as they follow Mayur back down the beach. When they're almost out of sight, I hear them laugh, and they start jogging again.

Martia begins to clear the tray. She always shakes her

head about the Bindas family and their big house and all the ornamentation that just exudes from their property, their green lawn. Even the rings on Mrs. Bindas's fingers and the bangles on her wrists. But Martia's careful around Mother. "Is good to see boys hungry," Martia says. "Polite, too," she adds.

"I'm surprised Mrs. Bindas encourages so many cousins to visit at once. I'm not sure Saco or Loco are positive influences on Mayur."

I roll my eyes when Kammi looks at me with raised eyebrows. For an artist, Mother is about as observant as a shark: she can't see what's right in front of her, but she can smell blood at a great distance.

Mother suddenly seems to remember Kammi and I are still standing there.

"Kammi, I see you have your supplies. Why don't you and I go inside? Still lifes make excellent studies, as Cyan properly noted. You want to make the most of your time here."

Kammi almost trips, she's in such a hurry to gather her materials and follow Mother inside. She doesn't seem to notice that I am not included.

CHAPTER TWENTY

ON THE twenty-third, early in the still-dark, before even Martia is up, I slip outside. Flip-flops, headscarf, T-shirt, and skirt. I know as I leave the house, feel the damp sea air on my arms, that this is not my usual scavenger walk down the beach. I know the date without looking at the calendar. I went to bed last night knowing and I woke up knowing.

June 23. A year ago today, Dad died. If I dreamed last night, I don't remember.

I clutch the key I borrowed from Martia's key ring. If I drop it in the sand, I'll never find it, not in the dark.

Shadows skitter along the sand. Not lizards, it's too cold at night. Their bodies don't hold heat. No, these are sand crabs. Scavengers like me, ghostlike at night.

The air feels so damp, maybe it's misting.

In front of me, the boathouse looms darker than the air around it. It looks like the entrance to a cave. I touch the peeling-paint walls, the indentation of the door—I think it's the door—and feel for the padlock. The metal chain is cold and wet. I trace my fingers down it like a blind person reading Braille. What if the lock has rusted through inside and the key won't work? What if no one can ever get in again?

The key fits, turns. I push and the bottom of the door scrapes along the sand, leaving a curved scar.

I climb into the boat. Where would he have put a note, if he left one? I run my hands along the lip of the boat frame, certain the police missed something. What do they know about anything? I search under the seats. Sometimes the Arabic-language teacher at school would tape a prize to the underside of a student's chair, a random surprise—a set of notecards, a book of children's poetry in Arabic, a package of date candies.

Nothing on the motor or under the anchor, the rope coiled on top. Nothing. Wait—a shard of broken glass under the seat. It's so sharp, and my hands so damp, maybe I cut myself. I grasp the sliver of glass anyway.

My eyes sting with salt. If he had drowned himself on purpose, he would have left a note for me, telling me not to worry. A note that said whatever happened had nothing to do with me. Wouldn't he? Isn't that what fathers are supposed to do?

Maybe the police found something after all and destroyed

it. Maybe Mayur's cousin pocketed a note and started rumors about it on the island. Maybe everybody knows but Mother and me. What if even Martia knows? Or what if Mother came the first night after they brought the boat in, and she was looking for the same thing, a note, some sort of evidence. Perhaps she found a note and burned it in one of the bonfires they lit on the beach for the returning search party. While everyone else seemed to care more about the body they were bringing in than she did. The flicker of scorched paper would have carried high on the wind like a prayer offering.

I lie in the bottom of the boat. The wooden ribs dig into my back as I press myself down. The planks still smell of the sea, even though the netting hangs long and dry along the walls. When I close my eyes, the boat seems to move up and down in rhythm with the waves pounding against the shore outside.

It seems to move, and I feel myself moving, too, as if I'm being tugged out to sea by the tide. I trace my fingers along the bottom, feeling for more clues.

That day, I stayed under the deck, my favorite hiding place away from the sun. Yet I was close to home, so I could sneak in to see what Martia was doing. Close enough to hear Mother and Dad above me, talking. That morning, Martia had packed a hamper for him and filled an ice bucket. I heard him ask Mother to come with him, to paint at sea.

She said no. She couldn't concentrate on art when the boat bobbed in the water. Having all that blue around her—

the sky, the sea, the boat itself—it was too intense, she said. I almost laughed and gave myself away. Too much blue? How could that be, when Mother surrounded herself with it? She couldn't even look at me without thinking of blue.

Dad's voice softened. He said it would be something she could do for him. Since he'd come all that way, after he'd stayed away for several summers, maybe this once she could go with him. He'd given up something, he said. What, I couldn't hear. Mother didn't answer him, but she didn't get up, either. Dad's footsteps echoed across the wooden flooring and steps. When he made it to the sand, his footsteps stopped making any sound at all. If he'd turned and looked down while he was on the deck, he would have seen me there. But he didn't. Above me, I heard Mother's steps, too. Only hers headed inside and stopped when the French doors closed.

From my hiding spot, I watched Dad moving toward the water. I didn't do anything that day but watch him go. Now, in my mind, I revise how it happened. I see myself scooting out from under the deck and running to catch him.

"Wait, Dad." I wave my arms. "I can go."

He turns, but it's almost as if he doesn't see me. He's looking up toward the widow's walk, looking for some-one else.

"Not this time," he says, smiling. "You hate fishing."

I watch him push the boat into the water, wade out knee-deep, until the blue boat clears the sandy sea bottom.

He hauls himself over the side, water spilling down his tanned legs. He lowers the motor into the water and turns away from shore, toward the open sea.

Even in my revision, he does not take me with him.

From outside, I hear something at the door. Something more than ghost crabs this time. I can't move. It wouldn't do any good anyway. There's only one way out. The window is bolted shut. Maybe it's just someone walking past the boathouse to fish in the surf. Maybe one of Mayur's cousins. Even from here, I can tell the sky is changing outside, lightening with the dawn. I close my eyes and cover my face with my scarf. It's still dark inside and there's no electricity. Maybe I'll look like an abandoned tarp.

The door squeaks.

"Cyan?"

Mother. If I don't speak, will she go away?

"I know you're here." Her voice is soft. I can barely hear her over the waves beyond. She must have watched me, then waited, certain there was nothing here for me to find.

"Couldn't you sleep?" she asks. I don't trust her voice. It's too soft. I wait for the snap. Part of me wants to say something. It wants to say no, I can't sleep. No, I can't get full.

"It hurts me, too. Don't you know that?" she asks.

She comes inside and closes the door. We're both in the dark.

I force my breathing to match the rhythm of the waves in the background. Not giving myself away. I want to say something, to tell her it was her fault. He shouldn't have been fishing alone that day. She should have gone with him. He'd still be with us if she'd gone.

"I loved your father, too. Nothing is ever as simple as you think it is, Cyan. You have to understand that." This is the most Mother has said about what happened in a year. For a whole year we have walked past each other, not talking about it. During that time, Mother decided she will marry another man. Even then we did not discuss what happened.

After a few minutes the door opens, letting in a moment of moon glow before it closes once more. The boathouse is again black inside, so dark my eyes see sparkles when I squeeze them shut and then open them wide. Just like that time in Hato Cave when the guide turned out the light.

They found Dad's boat the next day. The currents had carried it out. They pulled it onto the beach and found his body entangled in the fishing net underneath. He tried to pull himself out of the water, the police report said. They found microslivers of blue paint under his fingernails, and one nail had ripped off. They think that occurred before death. His shoulders and arms had been bruised. From the strain of trying to save himself? That was possible. Maybe fingernail scratches and not the netting itself or the anchor rope caused the blue paint to rub off in spots.

All the evidence suggested his death was accidental.

But the champagne bottle troubled the commissioner. That and the missing wineglasses. There was no alcohol in his body, though, the autopsy report said. He wasn't drunk. Nor were there any fish in the ice chest. A few shards of clear glass lay scattered in the bottom of the boat, along with a wineglass stem. Had the glass been broken on purpose? By accident? Where were the goblets?

They collected the evidence in a clear plastic pouch, except for the glass sliver I found just now. A tragic incident, the newspaper said the first day after. The police report used fewer adjectives. Its conclusions were vague.

"That's the way of all bureaucrats," Mother said as we waited at the airport to leave. "A way to angle money out of you as you wait for them to tell you something. When you can go. When you can take the body. I went straight to the American embassy. You can bet they moved faster after that."

I lie in the boat until light comes through the window. Dust motes float in the air like microscopic jellyfish. I brush my footprints away from the door when I relock it, and pocket the key. Covering up the evidence.

CHAPTER TWENTY-ONE

BACK AT *Blauwe Huis*, I slink to my room without seeing Mother. I pass by Kammi's door, careful to avoid the spot in front that squeaks. I save the sliver of glass in my box. It doesn't fit with the sea glass. It's too sharp and clear, and I'll cut myself on it if I forget it's there and run my hand inside the box. But there's no other safe place to keep it.

Martia doesn't hum or sing the whole day. She walks around the house silently, not even firing up the stove. We eat cold salad and sandwiches for lunch, almost as if it's a Sunday and Martia has gone home. For once, she doesn't tell us to fill up, to eat more.

Late in the afternoon, after listening to Mother pace upstairs in her studio, I hear her creep downstairs. She walks past Kammi, who's flipping through art magazines at the table, and me, lying on the jute rug, staring up through the clear glass coffee table, studying the undersides of the shells. She doesn't even look at me, much less mention the boathouse.

"Martia, please call a taxi," Mother says.

"Jinco, he is no working today."

"So call another cab. There must be someone else you know. We're going out to dinner."

Apparently, even Mother can't stand the silence of the house.

"Sí," Martia says.

Martia places the call from the kitchen, as if she doesn't want Mother hanging over her shoulder, criticizing which cab company she chooses.

When she returns, she says: "Twenty minutes. The cab, it is coming."

"Come with us," Mother says. She motions Martia closer.

Mother has never asked Martia to come out with us. If Martia's surprised, she doesn't show it. She raises her hand, pushing away the offer, as if Mother is just teasing her with the promise of an expensive meal in Willemstad.

I almost bang my head on the glass coffee table getting up. "Come on, please." Suddenly, I want Martia to come with us, more than anything else I've wanted this summer.

She smiles at me, a wistful smile, but she shakes her head. Her place is not with us there. Her place with us is only here, for one month, in a house that doesn't belong to any of us.

"Is better. You go to nice place, have a good dinner."

Even Martia wants us away on this day. She doesn't like the way the house feels any more than we do.

The shiny blue air-conditioned taxi arrives on time. Crisply dressed, the driver holds the door for Mother, something Jinco never does. The car is solid, expensive, with leather seats. Kammi scoots into the middle between Mother and me. She smoothes out her linen skirt and tucks her flower-print purse on the seat between us.

The driver smiles into the rearview mirror at Mother. His eyes never stray to look at Kammi or me. He knows who has the money. "Where are you going?"

"Otrobanda. Café Azul."

"Ah, yes, Azul, very good fish, shrimps, there." The man eases the car out of the driveway smoothly, not the way Jinco does, leaving a trail of dust everywhere.

"You are new here?" the driver asks.

"No, we come every summer," Mother says. She doesn't explain that this is Kammi's first visit.

"Oh, that is very good. You know where you are going. No need to point out the tourist sites."

"Thank you." Mother turns her head to look out the passenger-side window.

Kammi nudges me, points at the colors of the sky to the west.

I nod. The colors mean it will soon be dark. That night, Dad didn't return. Mother finally stopped pacing along the widow's walk and called the police to report him missing. I told her to tell them to check the airport. Maybe he'd taken the boat to Willemstad and then taken a plane back to Maine or Italy. Mother just told them Dad had gone out to fish and he hadn't come back. I sat outside on the deck growing colder and colder despite the tropical air until Martia wrapped me in a shawl and made me hot chocolate, the kind my grandmother used to make, with the miniature marshmallows on top. The locals—I don't know how they knew; maybe Martia summoned them like spirits—set bonfires on the beach, to provide a light should Dad be lost and unsure of the shoreline.

The trip to town takes forever with the traffic. Lights begin to twinkle on as the taxi driver winds down narrow streets, eases past slower cars, avoids pedestrians. Despite the crush, he never jerks the steering wheel. He'll charge Mother more than Jinco does, but she won't mind paying.

"Kammi, look over here," Mother says, pointing to the floating market.

"Remember? That's where the boats go, the ones that come from Venezuela for trade," I say. "The fishing boats." The words are out of my mouth before I can stop them.

Mother sucks in her breath.

Kammi unzips her purse, takes out a small map, and quickly unfolds it. I recognize it's a cruise-ship map, one we picked up in Willemstad on our previous trip. The map posts all the important tourist spots, or at least the shops that pay to have their names printed on the map. "The pottery place. May we go there? My mom—my mom likes pottery."

"Perhaps after dinner. I think there's a shoe shop in Otrobanda, too. You need hiking shoes."

Kammi says, "I'm sorry. I should have brought some."

"Nonsense, how would you have known? But I can't send you home with blisters on your feet."

I wriggle my toes in my flip-flops. I don't have hiking shoes, not even sturdy sports sandals. I left them in Maine.

Mother pays the taxi driver a partial fare, and he agrees to wait for us.

Café Azul looks out over the water. The waiter gives us a table right by the window. Mother motions Kammi into a chair close to the window and then sits opposite her. Leaving me to sit to the side, like an extra chair leg.

The air smells fresh, despite the grills going full blast in the kitchen.

Mother orders a Blue Bay for herself, sodas for us—mine a diet—not even asking what we want.

"Do you like spicy?" Mother asks Kammi.

"How spicy?"

"Pepper and lime, almost like a curry. Just a hint of hot. I recommend the mango fish platter. If it's as good as last year."

Mother dares to speak of last year.

"They have fish and chips," I say, pointing to the children's menu. Dad liked to go to fancy restaurants and order fried food. It was something he and Mother argued about.

"Fried food should be outlawed." Mother slips off her reading glasses, the rectangular ones, and folds them next to her plate.

After the waiter returns with our drinks, paper umbrellas propped against the glass rims for show, he takes our order. Mother and Kammi choose the mango fish. I ask for grilled fish with lemon, but with French fries.

Mother's smile stays tight, but she doesn't change my order for me.

While we wait for the food to arrive, I stare at the candelabras on the bar across the room. They are huge, ornate, as if someone stole them out of a cathedral. They look out of place here, in a restaurant with simple pale blue walls, cobalt trim, and white curtains.

"Are you going to do Mrs. Bindas's show?" Kammi asks, breaking the silence.

Mother shrugs. "I'd rather not. But I feel obligated. The Bindases have been nice to us for the last couple of years."

"I think it would be fun." Kammi dips a straw into her lime-colored drink.

"That's because you're just getting started." Mother gives Kammi hope with that sentence, that she thinks Kammi may have artistic abilities. Kammi grins.

"What was it Philippa said? About workshops?" I ask, knowing the answer.

Mother has to acknowledge I've said something. "Workshops provide income but no inspiration."

"I'd think it would be inspiring, helping people learn how to paint," Kammi says.

"Some people teach and then they have nothing left for their own art," Mother says, her voice harder than I bet she intends.

"Philippa's managing to do both." At least, that's what the postcard suggested—Philippa with her work for hire, but also with inspiration as large as Venice.

Mother's head jerks. "Ah, yes, Philippa." She says her name as if it is a sour fruit.

"Philippa. She was your favorite, wasn't she?" Kammi asks. I know she wants to be Mother's next protégé. How convenient that she will live with us. Philippa practically did toward the end.

The waiter brings our food, and Mother doesn't answer while he's jostling around us. When he finally leaves, I'm expecting her to change the subject.

But she twists a piece of bread in half and says, "Her passion. That's why she was my favorite."

Kammi wrinkles her forehead.

"She was willing to sacrifice anything for her art," Mother says. "Almost anything."

"Like what?" I ask. Philippa didn't seem like the sacrificing kind. She sometimes went to Italy to paint during the summers. She spoke Italian with Dad when she and Mother painted; I could hear them in the studio. She wore vintage clothes from an expensive boutique near campus.

Mother looks over as if she forgot I'm sitting here.

"Friendship." Mother butters her bread. "Happiness, even."

"How can art make you do that?" Kammi says.

"It makes you think of things you shouldn't," Mother answers. An honest answer, I can hear it in her voice. Something I haven't heard from her in a long time. I wonder what she means.

The waiter comes back to check on us. The moment is over, and we talk about things like the fish, how artful it looks on the plate, trimmed with bright fruits. I squeeze lemon over mine and devour the taste.

We skip dessert. Mother and Kammi say they're too full.

Outside, Mother speaks to the taxi driver. He agrees to meet us at the pottery store, a few blocks away, close to the import shoe shop. Tourists and locals alike crowd the sidewalk—I hear Dutch, Spanish, and Papiamentu. English, too.

At the shoe store, the assistant makes a beeline for Mother. She enters a business that way, demanding to be served without saying a word.

"Hiking shoes?" she asks.

The man, his face a question, repeats what Mother has said, as if he's sure he misheard.

"Hiking shoes, for the girls." Mother waves toward us.

"*Claro*," the man says, beaming. Somehow he knew the hiking shoes couldn't be for my mother.

He carefully measures Kammi's feet, produces a perfect hiking shoe with the first pair he brings out from the back room. She walks around on the carpet, flexing and pointing her feet one by one. She smiles.

"Now," he says, looking at my feet.

"Sports sandals, that's what I want," I say. "Not boots." I hate the idea of my feet being closed in. Even the thought of pebbles getting under my feet doesn't bother me as much.

Mother walks over, picks up a hiking boot off a shelf. "Are you sure—"

"Yes." I don't give in.

The man waits a second, but Mother doesn't respond.

"I have just the thing," he says, and he disappears into the back again.

The sandals fit. I pull the webbed straps close and secure them with Velcro. The rugged bottoms are ridged to grip the trail.

The taxi driver is parked right outside the pottery store when we walk up. He takes our packages and gets back in the car to wait for us.

Tourists cram the pottery store. A cruise ship has had engine problems, a clerk tells Mother, so the tourists have extra time for shopping. The clerk tucks a stray hair behind her ear, then dashes off to help a woman with a nasal Midwestern accent select local pottery. Mother rolls her eyes, but Kammi doesn't seem to notice. She holds her flower purse tight and marches up and down each aisle, every once in a while picking up a small bowl or plate, then putting it back on the shelf. Just before Mother starts to look at her watch, Kammi heads straight back to the first aisle and chooses two small bowls, which will be easy to pack and won't take up much room in her perfect suitcase. Each bowl is a rich brown with streaks of red bursting from the center outward. The sign says the design is called "Carnival."

"My mom likes brown and red together," Kammi says.

Blood and earth, I'm thinking. That's what those colors mean. Not chocolates and cherries.

On the ride back, Kammi holds the pottery package close on her lap. Mother doesn't speak, and neither do I. The air between us feels so heavy, not even Kammi speaks again, and the taxi driver turns up the jazz station on the radio as if to stir the air inside the car.

June 23 comes and goes, with no answers. Aside from the quiet moments in the boathouse, we didn't talk about the anniversary. We stalked the topic all day, never closing in. Mother and I were just like the lizards that circle each other sometimes on the wall of the house.

After Mother retreats upstairs and Kammi goes to her room, I open the French doors and sit on the deck. I almost believe that if I walked out onto the beach, I'd see the bonfires they lit that night, brighter than those from the Bindases' cookout. The sea beyond the white curve of phosphorescence along the shore is solid darkness.

The door to the widow's walk creaks open. That's all I hear, but I know Mother is there above me, alone in the dark. After I go inside, I close the door to my room, which is nestled against the back wall of the house, farthest from the sea. From here I can't even hear the waves.

A year, and I'm still hoping for clues.

What can Mayur know?

CHAPTER TWENTY-TWO

EXACTLY at seven on Saturday morning, Dr. and Mrs. Bindas arrive to pick up Kammi and me. Martia gives us each a backpack stuffed with snacks and a bottle of water. "Just in case," she says. Kammi struggles to fit in a portable watercolor board and her small case of paints.

The sun is already glaring at us when we step outside. The air smells dry and hot, as if we're not close to the sea.

Mother follows us to the SUV. She glances at my feet. I'm wearing the sports sandals, though I was tempted not to. I stashed a pair of flip-flops in my backpack for later.

Mrs. Bindas sits in the passenger seat. She presses the button to lower the window. From the driver's seat, Dr. Bindas holds his hand up to greet Mother. Very formal. "Good morning, Mrs. Walters," he says clearly, without emotion. Like he was at the beach party, he's proper, distant. Is that a trait of doctors in general or only of this doctor, because of who he is—or because of whom he declared dead on the beach? Whenever he sees Mother, he must see himself standing on the beach, still dressed in his fine clothes from a party, touching the white, white skin of a dead man he'd invited for cocktails or a dip in the pool that same week.

"No worries," he says as he unlocks the back, and I open the door. Kammi pulls herself in, lugging her pack behind her. I swing in after her and slam the door shut.

"The girls, they will be very safe," Mrs. Bindas says.

Mother looks past Mrs. Bindas to her husband, perhaps to confirm. Mother must have visions of Kammi sliding off a steep trail and landing in a ravine, where no one can reach her. She must worry that Howard will think she's been negligent and killed his only daughter. Maybe he'll think she's a dangerous widow, a woman who kills those closest to her. Maybe he'll break off the engagement.

"I've been on the trail many times before. At all times it is well marked," Dr. Bindas says.

"Where are the others?" Kammi asks. She means the boys—one boy, especially.

"The boys are still getting organized. They stayed up very late." Dr. Bindas frowns.

Mrs. Bindas turns in her seat and smiles at us, a big swept-up smile, just like her hair, though today she has tucked her hair under a red and gold scarf. She looks like a bright bird. "You will see. They are very interested to be going. After breakfast, I'll leave them to hike with Dr. Bindas."

Kammi smiles.

Kammi and I wave at Mother as we pull out. That is what families do.

Dr. Bindas swings the car wide into the shell driveway at their house, spewing shells onto the green lawn for the gardeners to pick out. Mayur and the other boys spill from the house, jostling each other, racing to see who will be last out. Mayur, since it's his parents' vehicle, steps to the SUV first, then flips the seat so that the others—Saco and Loco and Roberto—can climb into the far back. Mayur claims his spot by the window, slams the heavy door. The houseboy closes the gate behind the SUV, but he continues to stare after us. I look back at him until he sees me and turns away.

"Kammi, Cyan, you remember Saco?" Mrs. Bindas twists in her seat, waves toward the back of the SUV. Kammi smiles and flashes a glance backwards, too, then faces the front again. She barely seems to have looked, but I see from her face that she knows exactly where Saco's sitting. If she looks in the rearview mirror, she'll be able to stare right into Saco's eyes. Mayur isn't paying attention, not even to Kammi. He unknots and reties a climbing rope, even though no one mentioned climbing. We're supposed to be hiking only. Mayur is just showing off, as usual.

. . .

Dr. Bindas pulls off the road to Christoffel National Park, stopping at a restaurant tucked in a grove of divi-divi trees bent seaward. The boys run ahead and stake out two tables on the porch. They jockey for position, fighting over who will have the outer seats.

"Boys," Dr. Bindas calls after them as he walks ahead of Mrs. Bindas, Kammi, and me. Either they don't hear him or they're ignoring him. Kammi and I follow Mrs. Bindas, who doesn't seem to notice the boys, or the frown from the café owner, who pops outside at the noise.

"Girls, please to sit here?" Mrs. Bindas smiles as a waiter comes over and wipes off a table and chairs with a towel.

"Yes, ma'am," Kammi says, though I notice her look over to see where Saco is sitting.

I join her, though I want to get closer to the table where the boys are, too; closer to Mayur and his promise of informa-tion, whatever it is. He has his back to us, and I wonder if he did that on purpose, sat facing away. He knows I'm curious, that I can't help myself. He isn't going to make it easy. Typi-cal Mayur.

The waiter comes with extra help and they quickly feed us a hearty meal of eggs and confetti rice. Mrs. Bindas's driver comes to pick her up, and then the boys, Kammi, and I pile back into the SUV. Dr. Bindas puts it into drive, and we head toward the mountain in the distance.

Inside the park, Dr. Bindas drives past the first trailhead parking lot.

"The longer hike," he says.

"Yes, not the girls' hike," Mayur says, and the other boys laugh.

"Boys," Dr. Bindas says, drawing the word out. "The hike we're going on is even more scenic. We go right to the top."

Saco taps Kammi's pack. "What's in here?"

"My art supplies," she says quietly.

"What for?" Mayur asks. This is his hike. He wants everyone's undivided attention.

"I want to paint something for my dad," she says.

My chest twinges when she says that, it's so unexpected. I thought she'd say she's practicing for Mother. Somehow, that would be less painful than the answer she gives to Saco.

"And you?" Loco asks.

"No, I'm here to hike." And to talk to Mayur. I don't bother to explain that I don't paint. I stare at the scenery.

"But your mother expects you to paint?"

"No, she doesn't." She prefers that I not. She wants to keep the art for herself, to tell me what art is and isn't.

"Do you know how tall Mount Christoffel is?" Dr. Bindas asks, his eyes reflected in the rearview mirror.

The boys guess among themselves.

"More than three hundred meters," Roberto finally says.

Dr. Bindas laughs. "But how much more?"

"Three hundred and seventy-four," Kammi pipes up.

"Excellent!" Dr. Bindas smiles into the rearview mirror. I grin. The information must have been on the cruise-ship tourist map.

"Three hundred is close enough," Mayur mumbles.

"You would not say that if it were your allowance you were rounding down," Dr. Bindas chuckles.

"That's right." Saco laughs and punches his cousin in the shoulder.

The road begins to wind through greener underbrush and vines. Cacti grow in clumps. Mango trees, their leaves a dark green, stand out, taller than the surrounding brush.

At the next trailhead, Dr. Bindas parks the SUV.

"Before we go," he says, "two rules: Stay on the marked path. At the top, wait for everyone else. I have the lunch basket." Then he grins, and the boys pour out. Kammi slides out on my side and shoulders her backpack. The edge of the watercolor board sticks out the top, the cord stretching over it.

Dr. Bindas hands us each a copy of the trail map. "In case you get separated. But that is not to happen. Right, boys?" Dr. Bindas looks only at the boys when he says this.

On the map, a star marks the peak of Mount Christoffel. The trail rises along the backside of the hill.

"From the top, you can see the ocean," Dr. Bindas reminds us.

Roberto and Loco jog toward the trail, their packs flopping against their backs. Mayur stalks off after them. Scraping his boot in the dirt, Saco waits at the trailhead. For Kammi? Dr. Bindas leans against the SUV to retie his shoelaces in double knots, something Dad used to do before hikes.

"Come on," I say to Kammi. I want to catch up to Mayur.

She nods and follows me. Saco falls in next to her. Dr. Bindas stays a few steps behind us. Then his cell phone rings, and he stops to answer it.

My sports sandals don't keep my feet from getting dusty, but they give me good traction on the dirt and stones. I start up the trail, leaning into the ascent. If I hurry, I can catch up to Mayur. But once I do, how can I get him to tell me what he knows, or what his cousin is supposed to know? I don't trust him. He'd say anything just to make me think he's important. His father may be a respected doctor here, and his cousins may have to be polite to him because of it, but I don't.

Roberto and Loco climb out of sight. Mayur's in sight, not that far ahead of me.

"Hey!" I call after him, but he doesn't turn around.

I walk faster and feel my face getting warmer. My shirt is damp where my backpack hugs my shoulders. At the next switchback, I look up the trail to see Mayur right above me. He's stopped to look back down. He's twirling a twig between his fingers. He's breathing hard, and his pudgy face is red. He knows, though, that I was trying to catch up. I can see it in his eyes.

Part of me wants to tease him about how he's not first up the trail, about how Roberto and Loco are in better shape. I don't, though. I need him to tell me what he knows.

I take a swig of water from the bottle Martia packed for me.

"At the beach party, you said something. You said you know something."

He digs in his pocket for a candy bar, rips the paper off, and stuffs the candy in his mouth. He nods, chewing.

"Wineglasses . . ." he mumbles, talking around the candy.

"That was in the police report. All that information. The champagne bottle, the broken glass." I don't tell him I found a shard in the blue boat, something missed by the investigators.

He swallows.

"Was there a note?" I ask him.

"A suicide note?"

That's what I was thinking, but I say, "Any kind of note?"

He grins and starts hiking up the trail.

At that moment, I hate him. I want to push him off the side of the trail. He wouldn't die—it's not that steep—but he'd slide a long way, over clumps of ground cactus and stinging bushes. I'd watch him all the way down, and then I'd tie my scarf to the closest bush on the trail to mark the spot. I'd hike back to meet Dr. Bindas and tell him there'd been an accident. He would be shocked. Mrs. Bindas, too, when she heard later. Then Mayur would tell them I'd pushed him, just like I pushed him into the pool last year. And after they'd been so kind.

I grab his backpack from behind. "Tell me."

He wrestles out of my grasp and faces me. "What'll you do for me?"

"What do you want?" I hate that I even ask him that question.

"Oh, maybe it's not me who wants something," he says. He pushes my chest, but not too hard. If he hadn't been afraid, he might have touched my breast. Maybe that's what he meant to do.

"Yeah, right," I say.

Mayur's eyes narrow. I bet he thinks he's supposed to hold something over me, and sex is the only thing he thinks having power over a girl is all about.

I try another tack. "I don't think you really know anything. If you did, you'd tell me right now."

He laughs.

"Does my mother know?" I ask.

He sobers, seeming to think a moment before shrugging.

I step back. It's an answer and not an answer. If my mother does know, she hasn't told me. Why not? And if she doesn't know, should I share the information with her?

"How do you know my mother knows? If she knows, she'd tell me."

"Are you so sure?"

I jerk past him up the trail. I imagine I feel a hand touch my butt as I go by.

CHAPTER TWENTY-THREE

SWEATING feels good as I pound up the trail, leaving Mayur behind. I don't even look at the trees, the vines. I barely hear the sound of parrots or wonder what color they are. Now I know what Zoe means about running track. The sweating makes you start to feel good after a while. Not even my anger at Mayur takes that feeling away.

I don't catch up to Loco and Roberto. I see them, though, as the ascent becomes rockier and less vegetated. Roberto makes it to the top first, Loco close behind him. They raise their fists in the air like conquering heroes. Then they dart out of sight, probably to explore the surrounding views from the summit.

I'm next, breathing hard as I scuttle up the last rocky

section. On top of Mount Christoffel, I'm at the point far-thest from the sea on the island. From here, the ocean looks the same color blue as the sky. The trade winds stir the air, cooling my skin. A pebble tumbles down the rocks below. Instead of Mayur, I see Kammi pulling herself toward me, hunching slightly under the weight of the art supplies in her backpack. She has this streak of stubbornness I'm beginning to like.

"You didn't wait for me," she says.

This is the second time I've seen her angry with me. There's hope. She can get angry.

For the first time, I hold my hand out to Kammi, and it feels good when she takes it and scrambles up the last few feet to stand next to me. I see Mayur so far down the trail he looks like a speck—or a mountain goat. I laugh out loud. Saco is with him.

"What?" Kammi peers around me, looking into the dis-tance, but not down. From the angle she's looking, she'll never see Mayur.

"Mayur. There." I point down the rock face. "He looks like a mountain goat from here."

Kammi giggles. "I think I can see the horns on his head." She looks at me, and her pink skin seems darker from the sun and the hike, even though she's wearing a hat. But I still see she wants me to like her.

I laugh out loud again. Mayur, the goat boy.

I drink from my water bottle and motion to Kammi she should do the same.

"So where's Saco?" I ask.

She blushes. "He was walking with me."

"And?"

She shakes her head. "Nothing. He didn't do anything. He's nice. Mayur wanted to talk to him. So he told me to go ahead."

"Really? Talk about what?"

"Mayur didn't say." Kammi fidgets with her pack, sliding it off one shoulder. "But I wondered if it had to do with you."

"Hmmm. Maybe Mayur told Saco or Loco about what happened to my dad. I bet Saco would tell you," I say as it comes to me. I grab Kammi's arm. "Ask him. Will you?"

For the first time I want something from her.

"I'll ask," she says.

"Today," I say.

"Today."

I sit on a rock ledge in the sun while Kammi sets up her paints. She arranges the tubes of watercolors in a circle like a color wheel. She tears a sheet of paper from the pad and clips it to the board, fastening all four sides to keep the wind from lifting the page and making the paint run. Then she pours water into a plastic cup and plants it next to her on the ground. Holding four brushes of varying widths in her hand, she looks at me.

"I can't remember how to start," she says.

"Really?" Mother would have told her when they went out.

"Would you show me?"

"What makes you think I know how to paint?"

"I—I figured you'd know. You said—"

"You figured I'd know by osmosis or something? Or it's in my blood?" So many artist friends of Mother's have said the same thing when they've met me at a gallery show. They assume I have inherited artistic skills. Funny how Mother has never thought so.

Kammi shrugs. She looks very young. "You said you used to."

I did say that. "Okay."

She smiles.

Saco and Mayur crest the top of the trail.

"What are you painting?" Saco asks. He leans over Kammi's shoulder.

"I don't know yet exactly."

Mayur says, "How about lizards? They sun themselves on rocks."

He's talking about me. I stretch out my legs on the rock ledge.

Kammi doesn't take the bait. "I'm thinking more of a landscape. You know, like a photograph, to take home a good memory."

A good memory. I look away, out over the divi-divi trees

to the whitecaps far below. The sea stretching to the edge of the earth.

Mayur shrugs. "Trees? That's boring. Hey, Saco, let's get the Hackey Sack."

"You brought that?" Kammi asks.

Saco shrugs and grins. "You brought art."

Saco loosens his pack and retrieves a small crocheted beanbag. He uses his foot to toss it in Mayur's direction, and Mayur kicks it up in the air, then steps back to let Saco move in and keep it moving.

"Don't fall off a cliff," I call after him. I don't have my answer yet.

The boys pass the Hackey Sack back and forth as they jog around the flat, rocky area.

I get up and stand behind Kammi. "Hold still." I put my hands on her shoulders, pulling them back and down. "Relax. You're too tense. I thought all you skinny girls took yoga."

"I'm not skinny." Holding her watercolor board, Kammi snaps her head to look back at me.

"Yes, you are." I nudge her head back toward the board in front of her. She looks at the blank paper clipped to it.

"First, don't look at the paper." I point toward the horizon. "Out there, that's where you should keep your gaze." Where the sea and the sky become one. Artists call it the vanishing point. For me, it's the place to start to focus, to find the line between what is and what isn't yet.

Dr. Bindas, who's reached the top, nods and smiles as he passes by. He doesn't say anything, though, as if artists deserve special reverence because they aren't like other people. Maybe that's why he still addresses my mother formally. Or maybe it's because he knows something about what happened.

"Hey," Kammi says, bringing me back. "If I don't look at the paper, how do I know what to paint?" Her voice rises. She shakes the brush she's holding.

"If you look at the paper, you're looking at the wrong thing. You're not seeing, not translating at all. You're faking it. It won't be as good. It won't be real."

Kammi turns to look at me. "Your mother looks at her canvas. She draws a faint line across it before she even starts."

I nod. "She's setting the Golden Mean, dividing her canvas." Anchoring herself. Mother doesn't trust that she will know where she is by instinct.

"Maybe you should start with drawing," I say. Mother's mantra.

Kammi shakes her head, her small mouth set. "No."

I smile, but she can't see me.

"Okay. Just remember, you wanted to paint landscape. Keep your eye on the horizon. Hold your brush against the dry paper."

"But the sea's so far away."

"Why do you think this is about painting the sea?" I ask.

Kammi looks at me and frowns.

I stretch my arms. "What's all that? In front of you?"

"The whole park?"

"Sky, stupid," I say, and laugh, but not hard. Not laughing at her. "It's all sky. There, just at the very edge of the earth, the sea even becomes the sky. That's it."

Under her bangs, her eyes stare straight through me, as if she thinks I've played a long practical joke on her. As if I've somehow tricked her into lugging her supplies all the way up here to paint the sea from a great distance.

Finally, when I don't laugh and say the joke is on her, she turns to look where I pointed, out toward the horizon. She leans closer to the paper. She reaches out and splats the brush on the paper, misjudging where it is in relation to her hand, extended by the length of the brush. She steadies herself and holds the brush lightly against the paper this time, barely making contact. Touching it like a blind person.

"Paint what you see," I say.

"There's no paint on the brush."

"I know. It doesn't matter yet. You're seeing it."

Kammi drops her arms to her side, the brush limp in her fingers. "I can't do that."

"Yes, you can."

"It's silly."

I throw up my hands. "It isn't. I won't laugh. Some of my best paintings have been done this way."

"You *are* making fun of me. You said you don't paint."

"I don't. Doesn't mean I haven't. Come on, this way there's no evidence." I use that word again, "evidence." I soak a small sponge in water, squeeze it almost dry. "Okay, before you start, we'll do wet on wet."

"What?"

"It's a watercolor technique. Mother didn't tell you this already?"

Kammi shakes her head.

"In watercolor, you can use dry paper and wet paint, dry paper and dry paint, and wet paper and wet paint. By dampening the paper and then painting, you soften the line, the tone. You'll like it." I move the sponge across the paper, quickly, but with long, even strokes. "Okay, now dip your brush in the water."

"Which one?"

"The wide one first. Always."

Kammi follows directions.

"Tap it on the edge. Get rid of the excess water." I watch her flick water onto the dry earth. "Lightly dip your brush in the cerulean blue. See just there at the horizon, where the pink hasn't burned off yet? Lightly dip the corner of the brush into the alizarin crimson. Now broadly lay in the sky from top to bottom."

Kammi's hand moves to the paper.

"Wait, don't try to come at it like a mouse. You have to mean it when you lay the paint down. Mean it, but hold the brush loosely. Like a boy's hand." I tease her. And she laughs. When her brush touches the paper, her strokes flow.

"So?" Kammi asks when she's finished, still holding the broad brush in her hand, the paint drying on it.

"What?" I take the brush and plop it into the cup of water. I know what's she asking, but I refuse to admit it.

"What now?"

"Now let it dry a little, not completely. Then you can tackle the sea. If you don't wait long enough, you'll ruin it. The paints will run, muddying up everything."

Kammi waits, then takes a thinner brush and dips it into the same cerulean.

I sigh. "Did you look at the sea?"

She squints.

"Is it the same blue?" I ask.

"No," she says, her voice low as she skims her palette for the right blue. "This one?" She points to the cobalt.

"Darker, the water will be a shade darker, and patchier, like the waves."

She bends over her work, her shoulders tense around her ears.

"Shoulders down," I say in her ear.

She obeys and keeps working. When she's finished, she cleans her brush.

"How's the painting?" she asks me directly.

"Do you need me to say it's okay?"

"Yes," Kammi says.

"It's okay so far."

Her face wilts.

"Really," I say. "It's good for a first attempt. You captured the mood, the bright morning, with a hint of darkness." Like the day. I untie my backpack and shuffle my feet into flip-flops, leaving the hiking sandals to breathe. "But you know, an artist wouldn't care what anyone else thought."

"Your mother does, and she's an artist."

Kammi has me. To the world, Mother is an artist. She gauges herself by what the critics say. She can close herself off in a dark room just waiting for the critics to write reviews in the art magazines. Before they've sounded the first weak note of praise, she's barricaded herself.

Do I care what people say about my jewelry? I've shown it only to Zoe, and not even everything. I have my own version of the inner sanctum, of turning the canvas from others' view. Maybe I'm no artist after all.

"Lunch!" Dr. Bindas calls us to the small, shady area near a rock outcropping where some scraggly divi-divi trees struggle to grow. Roberto and Loco are already there. Mayur and Saco scoop up their Hackey Sack and come running. Why they brought it with them on the hike I have no idea. Except that they wanted to show off for Kammi; that's clear. She was looking at Saco out of the corner of her eye when she was supposed to be painting. Maybe it worked.

CHAPTER TWENTY-FOUR

"REMEMBER to ask him," I tell Kammi as we join Dr. Bindas and the boys for lunch.

She nods. Saco's left half a blanket open next to him, and Kammi takes it, sitting delicately with her feet tucked to the side, arranging herself like a model posing for an artist. No one tells her how to do this, she just knows by instinct.

I take a space at the edge of Dr. Bindas's blanket, close enough to Mayur to catch his eye if he looks my way. The boys eat noisily, like feasting crows.

After lunch, Dr. Bindas says he's going to take a nap, he's tired from a late night at the hospital. He finds a patch of shade and lies down. Once he's been still for a while, Saco stands and nods toward a trail. We all, even Kammi, make our way over. When I look back, Dr. Bindas hasn't moved.

"There's a short trail this way," Saco says.

"Where to?" Kammi asks.

"A cave," Mayur says, flapping his arms like a bat's wings. Kammi shivers.

"It's not dangerous," Saco says, frowning at his cousin.

"I don't see a cave on the map." I hold the paper map Dr. Bindas gave us in front of me.

"It's not on the official map," Saco says. "But I've been there before. It isn't far. It's about here." Saco points to a blank space on my map. "We brought flashlights."

Kammi and I don't have flashlights. Caves are one thing Martia didn't prepare us for today.

"Are there bats?" Kammi asks.

"Not last time. It's not like the sea caves," Saco says.

"Won't Dr. Bindas get mad if he wakes up?" Kammi asks.

"Not at you." Loco grins.

The thought of going to a secret cave that isn't on the map excites the boys. I can feel their desire to sneak off fan out in hot, dry waves across my skin.

"We can go quickly and come back. We'll stay together," Roberto says.

Mayur looks at me. "If you come, it will be worth it." Does he mean he'll tell me?

Saco looks at Kammi, who turns to me.

"Okay." I nod. If we're with the boys, Dr. Bindas can't say we were hiking alone.

The cave is farther than I thought it would be. I'm still wearing my flip-flops, but the sports sandals are in my pack. I bring up the rear, easing my way around prickly pear cacti.

If this is a trail, it's a wild donkey path.

I'm sweating, and the sun glares down on us. Did Dr. Bindas wake up yet and wonder where we are? We didn't leave him any clues. Not even a stack of rocks pointing the way we walked. Just Kammi's painting drying in the sun.

"This is it," Saco says, pointing. An overhang of rock hides the cave entrance. I'd never have seen it.

The boys dig flashlights from their packs. Saco has two. He gives one to Kammi, who looks at me. I shrug.

"I have an extra one, too," Mayur says. "Maybe the batteries will last." He hands me a skinny flashlight, the kind that uses double-A batteries. I press the button and hold my hand over the front to shield the sunlight. A faint glow shows it's working, though how bright it will be inside, I don't know.

Roberto, the oldest, goes first. Mayur could have insisted he go first like he usually does, but I think he's afraid.

Loco goes second, then Saco, with Kammi right behind him. Saco reaches behind and puts his hand on Kammi's head to make sure she crouches far enough not to hurt herself going through the entrance.

"You go," Mayur says.

"No, you." No way I'm letting him follow me into the darkness.

"Afraid?"

"Not of the cave," I say.

If he's disappointed, he doesn't show it. He just shrugs and ducks inside. I could turn back now. I know the trail back to the picnic area. I could find Dr. Bindas.

I take a deep breath and step into the shadows. The cool air flows toward me from deeper inside the cave, and I can smell the darkness. I didn't know before that darkness has a scent. I touch the wall. Rough limestone, it feels chalky, yet almost damp, like a tray of oil pastels. From somewhere, separate from the voices of boys, I hear the trickling of water.

After a few steps, the outside world seems far away. Here, inside, the air feels heavy, pressing against me. The flashlight shines, but its narrow beam only illuminates the tiniest area in front of me.

Suddenly, something screeches. Wings flutter around my ears. I duck.

"It's okay," Roberto calls as the noise dies away. "It's just an owl. They nest in caves sometimes."

My knees shake a little as I stand again and follow Mayur.

"There's a hole just here, be careful," Roberto calls back, his voice distorted. Flashlight beams cut across the cave like airport spotlights.

I stay close behind Mayur. Even though he's short, he

still has to stoop as we go farther into the cave. I run my hand along the ceiling so I won't bump my head on any out-croppings.

I follow him around the dark spot on the cave floor. The hole. I wonder how far down it goes, and my stomach flips.

"So, tell me," I say.

"Wait."

"Why? The secret's not in here, is it?"

Mayur laughs. "Maybe. And there are things best talked about in the darkness. Secret things."

A chill goes through me, but I think it's just the cool temperature inside the cave.

His hand brushes my skirt. I imagine he's reaching out to touch the wall.

"Come see, it's not much farther. At the back of the cave, you can stand up." Roberto's voice echoes. I can't tell how far away he is. "And there's a little hole in the top."

Someone shrieks. Just ahead of us. A girl?

"Kammi?" My own voice rises. What if she falls? It'd be my fault. I told her it would be okay. My hand reaches out in the darkness, as if I might feel her in front of me. Someone or something brushes my fingers, and I'm not sure if it's Mayur or someone else or a bat that Saco says doesn't live here. I jerk my hand back.

Saco answers, "It's okay, she just slipped a little. Watch out—there's water in a couple of places."

I slide my flip-flops along the cave bottom to avoid stumbling.

Suddenly, we're in the chamber and we can stand up straight. A thin light shines through a hole in the cave's high ceiling.

"Hey, see the drawings?" Loco shines his flashlight on the wall.

"Are they native?" Kammi asks.

Saco laughs. "The natives didn't draw *corazones*, hearts."

I see graffiti with people's initials.

"There's more," Roberto says, and he and the others move to the far end of the chamber. Saco shadows Kammi, as if he's protecting her.

Mayur stands close to me. This is my chance, here in the cave. I touch his arm. "Now."

He whispers "Maybe" as he finds my hand, the one that touched his arm, and pulls me to kneel on the cave floor with him. My heart starts to pound. I can't see his face. He turns off his flashlight.

He runs his hand across the top of my skirt until he's touching my T-shirt.

I grab his hand and cut off my flashlight. I don't want anyone to see me.

"What are you doing?"

"You want to know what I know? Kiss me." I smell his skin, its musky scent not that of a little boy's. He takes shallow breaths, as if he's afraid to inhale a deep swallow of cave air. Maybe he thinks it's poisonous. Caves can be that way, with pockets of poison gas, and we're close to the floor, where bad air settles.

His other hand finds my shoulder. He runs a finger across my collarbone.

The air is so heavy, like water. I can't breathe. I wonder where the others are, whether they can see us in the darkness.

"You don't even like me," I say. Not the way Saco likes Kammi.

"You're a girl. An American girl." He says it as if that's enough reason. I'm an American girl, so I'm easy. I want something from him. He wants something from me.

He leans closer. I hold my breath. Behind my closed eyes, I see stars on a black canvas. He kisses my neck, letting his tongue explore that indented place below my throat. I hope he tastes salt.

"There was a note," he says, and then kisses more of my throat. His hands touch my shoulders now and inch downward toward my chest.

I knew Dad wouldn't have left me without telling me it wasn't my fault. "Where?"

"His book." Mayur puts a hand under my shirt. I can't move. I'm waiting for each word to drop out of his mouth like a jewel.

"The note?" I ask. I'm confused. In what book? The one

Dr. Bindas returned to us, *The History of Language*? Mayur's hand brushes the top of my left breast over my sports bra. In the cold, his hand feels warm over my skin. I hate that it feels good, that I want his hand there so he'll keep talking. "It— the note," he whispers, his breath catching as his hand moves. "The note in his book. He left by the pool."

Dad was in the sea for more than twenty-four hours. All that time Mayur had the note.

"What did it say?" I ask. Mayur's lips touch mine, almost by accident. They move past to my cheek, then return.

He shifts closer. "It wasn't your father's."

The blood goes out of my head. "I don't understand. What do you mean? Not his note?"

Mayur's lips touch mine again. He presses toward me.

I jerk back.

"Maybe you don't want to know any more?" Mayur asks, his voice husky.

I want to know. I make myself kiss his cheek. The cave air pushes against me.

"He didn't write it." Mayur runs his hand under my bra. No boy has ever touched me there. The closest is when a boy in my class nuzzled my neck while playing spin-the-bottle at a party in seventh grade. I didn't even tell Zoe. "It was written *to* him."

"Mother wrote it?" Was it a farewell letter from Mother, asking for a divorce? Saying that she'd met Howard and she wanted to leave Dad? That would explain why she didn't tell me about the letter. She'd feel guilty if Dad died with a note like that in his possession. She knows I'd hate her.

Mayur doesn't answer. He's too busy exploring the curves of my chest. He lifts my shirt and, pulling my bra aside, kisses one of my breasts. He runs his tongue over the surface, and I shudder, turning my head away.

"Are you here?" A voice—Saco's?—sounds far away.

I don't answer. Mayur doesn't, either. I don't want them to come back now. I want more time.

"Tell me." And I push my breast hard into Mayur's soft mouth. He sucks softly, and my body wants more.

He draws back. "I like that." He runs his hand over my wet breast, brushing it lightly, teasing.

"That is the mystery," he says. "It's not a note from your father or your mother."

I hear the others coming back. Mayur reaches over and pulls my bra down over my breast, as if I'm incapable of covering myself.

I can't even speak. I don't know what to think. The note was in the book Dad had been reading. Then why didn't Dr. Bindas turn it over to the police? Nothing makes sense.

"Why didn't your father give it to the commissioner?"

"He didn't know about the note. I found it."

I imagine Mayur thumbing through Dad's book. Touching the pages with his guilty boy fingers. Finding a note creased inside. Hiding it. Keeping it secret.

"A note. So what? Maybe it wasn't anything. Maybe it was just a receipt from a bookstore." I feel my voice going higher. I don't want Mayur to think the note is important.

"Part of it was written in Italian," Mayur says.

"Dad taught Italian. He was an Italian *professor*." It was a letter from a student or from the university in Rome where he researched.

"It was a love letter. From a woman."

"What did it say?"

"It's a quote from some artist. Chagall. Something about there's only one color in life, the color of love. Then the rest is 'I love you' in Italian. Over and over."

Mayur backs off now that he's delivered his news, as if he's embarrassed to talk about words of love, even in a dark cave where we can't see each other's eyes.

"Hey, what's going on?" Saco shines his light on us.

Roberto chuckles. "Oh, ho, Mayur, I didn't know."

"Who?" My voice sounds raspy. "What's her name?"

Mayur seems to not hear them. He speaks only to me.

"Pippa," he says.

Pippa.

Suddenly, I am very cold. Behind my closed eyes, I see stars again. I can't breathe.

"Give it to me." Mayur's lying. He doesn't have a note.

Mayur turns on his flashlight. The beam jiggles as he pulls a piece of paper from his front pocket. He unfolds it. I can't read it in the semidark, but when the light shines over the signature at the bottom, I can see it's real. I can see the way Pippa's "p's" intertwine and loop back around her name. Mayur couldn't fake that signature, couldn't even know it.

I snatch the note from his hand. The thin paper tears in my fingers.

Kammi touches my arm. "Cyan, are you okay?"

"Let go of me." I yank away from Kammi, her hand on my arm reminding me of Mayur. I squeeze the note in my hand. "Don't touch me. Leave me alone."

I spring to my feet and run back toward the entrance, which glows like the moon across open water. I just keep running toward it. I don't even turn my flashlight back on.

"Stop!"

"Watch it!"

Voices shout behind me like bad spirits. Slaves used these caves for voodoo ceremonies, I read that somewhere. Or maybe Martia told me. She said she wouldn't go in caves. She's superstitious.

It's my fault. I came here. I feel the dampness where Mayur's mouth touched my skin, and I feel sick.

The ground goes out from under me. The moon disappears, and I feel myself falling. My shoulder slams against rock. The flashlight flies from my hand. I don't know up from down. Something rough scrapes my head, and I lose my left flip-flop. The backpack I'm wearing slams against a hard surface. Then the back of my head hits the ground.

CHAPTER TWENTY-FIVE

I'M LYING FLAT and I don't feel anything. Except for my head. It hurts.

I wake up again. Or maybe it's for the first time. My head is hot, but everything else feels cold. I lie there, breathing. I'm no longer falling. The world spins the way it does after a ride at a fair.

When I open my eyes again, I blink to make sure they're open. The darkness is the same as when my eyes are closed.

The silence presses against my chest, reminding me of Mayur, of his body against me. I try to move a little. A toe, an ankle, the other leg. My shoulder twinges. I'm lying on my backpack, and it digs into my muscles. I roll over a little and then gag from the nausea. I slip the backpack off and lie down again.

I don't know how long I've been here. Or how far I fell. Or where the others are. Did they leave me?

I imagine Mayur somewhere nearby, telling his cousins how I let him touch me. How he held my breast in exchange for a secret. Maybe Roberto teases him, saying he didn't get enough for his secret. Maybe they're laughing. Maybe not Saco.

"Hello?" My voice comes out, but it sounds like a whisper even to my own ears.

No answer. I run my hands beside me, trying to find the flashlight.

The note, too, is gone. Knocked from my hand.

I have to find the flashlight. Then I can find the note. Above, I can see only a faint patch that's less black than everywhere else. That must be the way out. I can't tell how high it is, though, or how far away.

Feeling the ground for the flashlight, I take off my right flip-flop. The other one I lost when I fell. The sports sandals are in my backpack. I can use them when I get out. On all fours, I inch my way closer to where I can see the faint spot.

"Hello!" This time, I shout toward the spot.

From far away, I hear a faint hello. They didn't leave, I think. Then I realize it's just an echo. The hello is my own voice coming back at me.

My head still hurts, so I lie back and rest. I feel better knowing I can open my eyes and see the way out, even if I can't yet reach it. I think about what Mayur told me.

Pippa is Philippa's nickname. She and Dad spoke Italian when she came to paint. Mother didn't know then that Philippa liked Dad, did she? When she practically lived with us?

"Philippa was willing to sacrifice almost anything for her art," Mother said to Kammi at Café Azul. It wasn't true, though. She sacrificed her art for something forbidden. She was my mother's best student. Did Dad love her back?

All this time I thought Mother was wrong, that she'd been having the affair. *Affair.*

I feel like I'm going to throw up. I gag, but I move my head. I ease my way along the cave floor, making sure there's not another hole I can fall through, until I feel a wall. I drag my backpack with my other hand. Inside, I still have the water bottle and some snacks. The pastries are probably crushed, but they'll taste just as good if I feel hungry again. I can't tell what time it is. I sit upright, wobbly, my legs shaking.

I feel so stupid. How did Philippa and Dad get together? Did Dad hate himself but Philippa's soft touch made him warm and he couldn't stay away? Who acted first? Did Dad see her painting in the sunlight, and he touched her hair and then he couldn't forget? I think of Mayur's hand in the darkness. I retch.

From very far away, I hear voices. This time, I know they aren't just echoes of my own voice. Above me, flashlight beams dart like searchlights.

"Cyan?" It's Kammi's voice. I hear the fear in it. She thinks I'm dead.

"Cyan?" Saco's voice penetrates the darkness.

"I'm here," I say. "Here!" I say it louder. The sound echoes in my brain when I talk that loud.

"I hear her. I hear her!" Kammi is shouting. Even from down here, however far I slid and fell, I can hear her relief.

"Are you hurt?" Saco asks.

"Not bad," I yell.

The light reaches me. I blink.

"You fell in the hole," Saco says. "We thought you'd run outside."

I remember now. I wasn't looking. The only thing that mattered was getting out of the cave.

"How long?" I have no idea.

"Thirty minutes, at most. We can't see you. Can you stand up?"

"Yes." I move. At first, my muscles don't do what I want them to. My leg muscles shake, my arms, too. I wait for the dizziness to pass, then stand.

It's then that I start to shiver.

"I lost the flashlight," I say. If they go away, I'll be in the dark completely. "Don't leave me here."

"We won't leave you," Kammi says. She speaks to someone else, but I hear her. "Where's your rope? Give her a flashlight. We can lower it down."

"Not my flashlight," says Mayur.

"Give it to her," Roberto says. "We'll share mine. We've got to figure out how to get her out of there."

I hear Saco again. "Cyan, the light, it's coming. Can you see it?"

I sit there looking up, the darkness spinning. I see the aluminum tube jerking down through the hole at an angle. I can see now that the cave wall slopes some; that's why I didn't fall straight down. Why I didn't break my neck.

"Yes."

"Okay, once you get it, take a look around. See if there's a way out from there."

With shaking hands, I untie the flashlight and turn it on. Now that there is a glimmer of light, I can breathe. I shine the light in a circle around me. There's a dark opening along one wall, but it looks black as pitch, blacker than the rest of the cave. Probably the hole goes farther down; maybe that's where the water seeps through to the rocks below.

"No, I don't see anything." I hear my voice rise again.

"Okay, it's okay," Kammi says.

The voices talk above me.

"We have a plan," Saco says after a minute. "We're sending the rope down again. This time, tie it around you, under your arms. Knot it twice. We're going to pull you back up."

I don't say anything.

"Cyan, are you there?" Kammi yells.

"I'm here." They want me to let them pull me back up through the hole I fell through once already. What if they drop me? What if the rope breaks? I rest my hand against the wall. I try not to think. I have to get out of the cave. There is only this one way.

"It's a real climbing rope. Very strong," Mayur says. I hear the pride in his voice. His bragging voice again.

The rope slithers toward me. I take off my backpack, loop the rope twice around my chest, and then knot it three times. I slide the pack onto my left shoulder, the one that's less sore, and stare up through the hole.

"Ready?" Saco asks.

"Wait." I shine the light around me, looking for the note. The evidence. I can't find it. I swing the light in wider circles.

"What are you doing?"

I don't answer. The white paper should glow in the light. Maybe it fluttered into the deeper hole. I can't see it.

"Cyan?" Kammi asks.

"I'm ready," I say. I hold the flashlight against my chest. The note is gone. Whatever happens, though, I won't let go of the flashlight.

"We see you. Check the knot."

I jerk it hard. It holds fast. "It's good."

"Okay, we're going to start. Slowly."

I feel the rope tighten around my chest. What if I can't breathe? What if it slips over my arms and I fall again? My stomach heaves.

"Are you okay?"

"Don't drop me."

"We won't. Hold the rope above the knot." Saco's voice is steady.

I grasp it with both hands, twisting it. "Wait." The rope stops. I stash the flashlight in the backpack. I'm too afraid of dropping it.

"Okay."

The rope tightens, and I'm moving. I almost can't breathe. I bump against the sloping wall, and the rope burns against my skin. Finally, my back rests solidly against the cave wall, and I'm being dragged up through the slanted tunnel.

The rope slips, and I let go to dig my fingernails into the sides of the tunnel. "Don't drop me."

"It's okay," Saco says. "The rope gave a little. No harm. We've got you. We can almost reach you. Hold out your hand."

I raise one arm above me into nothingness. The rope tugs me a few more inches.

Hands grip my arm, hard. I don't mind. They pull me the rest of the way out of the hole. They leave me lying there, gasping like a fish out of water. Is this how Dad felt, trapped in the netting under the blue boat? Could he see the sky above the water but not reach it because of the weights holding the net down? He clawed with his fingernails against the wooden boat, but that didn't save him. The police report mentioned blue paint chips under his nails. He must have tried to save himself. He didn't want to die. He died so close to the surface, so close to the light, yet he couldn't breathe.

I feel myself start to cry.

He came to Curaçao last summer for a reason. Even with the note in the book he was reading, he asked Mother to go out in the boat with him. He brought champagne. You don't offer champagne to ask someone for a divorce. No one would do that. Dad wouldn't do that. He came to make up, to put the past behind them. He didn't leave Mother or me on purpose.

"You're okay," Kammi says. "Everything's okay."

Mother refused to go with him. Does that mean she wanted a divorce? Had she known all along? Kammi's parents are divorced, but there are worse things. There are worse secrets.

"Can you get up?" Mayur asks. Now his boy voice sounds worried. Maybe Dr. Bindas has already called the police. Maybe Mayur's worried I'll tell his father about how he touched me. I won't, though. I wanted him to tell me. I wanted him to touch me.

"Yes." My voice comes from somewhere.

"Let me help you," Loco says. He and Roberto both help me up, and they untie the rope. My muscles are starting to ache. My head buzzes. But I'm going to be okay.

Outside the cave, I blink in the harsh light, unable at first to focus. I inhale deep, long breaths. Glad to be alive.

Kammi speaks first. "You look awful!" Then she clamps

her hand over her mouth. They don't teach that in Atlanta, to be so frank.

I touch my head. There's a small bump.

Mayur groans. "Can we just say she slipped on the trail?" He refers to me as if I'm not standing there, as if we didn't touch in the cave.

"You mean not tell Dr. Bindas what happened?" Kammi's mouth drops open.

"It might be best," I say as I look down at my dirty arms and scraped skin. I don't want to disappoint Dr. and Mrs. Bindas. I don't want to tell Mother what happened. "Except I'm covered in mud."

"There's a stream back there. We can say you fell near it," Loco says.

"And that you slid, and we had to pull you up with the rope." Mayur's into his story. I wonder if he knows my fantasy earlier of pushing him off the trail.

CHAPTER TWENTY-SIX

IN THE END, we tell Dr. Bindas everything. Well, not everything. Just about the forbidden cave and my fall. As soon as Kammi mentions my accident, Dr. Bindas goes into medical mode. Making me lie down, he even forgets to be angry, forgets that he yelled at us, shaking his cell phone in his hand as if he tried to call us. He checks my pulse and my eyes to see if I have a concussion. He feels both arms and legs, searching for breaks. These are injuries he can do something about.

Satisfied I'm mostly okay, he stands and helps me up.

"We're walking down now. Boys, single file. In front of me, so I can see you." Dr. Bindas is starting to act angry again; I can hear it in the way his voice darkens now that the panic is over.

We walk slowly, stopping every fifteen minutes to make sure I'm okay. I don't mind. My whole body is becoming so sore, I can't walk any faster. Dr. Bindas makes Mayur carry my ruined pack. Martia won't be able to get it clean again.

Mayur and I don't talk about why I ran and fell. Some secrets are best kept.

Once when we stop, Kammi asks me what happened, what Mayur told me. She holds her watercolor in front of her so it doesn't smudge.

"There was a note."

With her free hand, Kammi squeezes my arm. She thinks I mean a suicide note. "It's not that, not what you think." I'll tell her the rest later—some of it, anyway.

Mother's waiting when Dr. Bindas drives up to the house in the SUV. All the boys sit in the back, quiet as shadows. I don't remember Dr. Bindas calling her, but he must have. She doesn't react when he explains to her in a low voice what happened, or when I wince getting out of the vehicle. She stands there stiff, her face stone. No hysterical mother blaming the boys. She doesn't even speak to Kammi, though I know she's relieved Kammi isn't the one hurt. Mother just wants to get us all back to the U.S. safely. When she looks at me, can she see that I know about Philippa? I wonder how much she knows. Or whether she can see that a boy has touched me.

As soon as the Bindases drive away, Martia takes charge, helping me to my room. She spoils me. All the coconut treats

I can eat, until I feel sick. Then she flutters around, checking my eyes again to make sure I don't have a concussion.

"Your mother, she worry about *mala cabeza*. Your headache."

"It doesn't hurt," I lie. But it's not that bad, just a dull ache.

Kammi hangs out on my bed, thumbing through art magazines.

"Why don't you show Mother your painting?" Since the day Kammi arrived, she's wanted to win Mother's approval.

"Maybe later." She says she stuck it in her closet, to hide it.

In the evening, Martia brings me chicken soup. Kammi spoons rice into the bowl to thicken the broth. She shakes her head, though, when Martia offers her a bowl. She holds up a piece of bread. "Not really hungry." As if she's the one who fell, not me.

After Martia leaves, Kammi leans closer. "What about the note?"

I inhale the warm scent of soup, its hint of lime. I re-member the way the darkness smelled, and I think of the note on the cave bottom, where no one will find it before the frag-ile paper disintegrates.

"It wasn't a suicide note," I say.

Kammi waits, her head cocked, expecting me to say more. Maybe I will someday, but not now. I don't want to tell her about my father and Mother's student. "It was a love note." That's all I say, not who it was from or for. I let her think what she will.

Mother knocks on the door, and Kammi backs away from me, blushing, as if she's been caught in a lie.

"Come in," I say.

"I didn't know you were here," she says to Kammi.

"Just visiting." Kammi sits very straight on the bed. I imagine her trapped between us like a rabbit between two cats, hoping that by freezing she'll escape notice.

"Martia says you're feeling better," Mother says. "I wanted to see for myself." She doesn't come any closer to the bed.

I make myself answer. "Yes. Better."

We haven't talked about how we feel in a long time.

"You frightened me. Both of you. Taking a risk like that," she says. "Following those boys into the cave. After what's happened."

After Dad happened, she means. But she still can't say it. After he slid under the dark water and didn't resurface. For a second, I can't breathe for remembering the cave, the blackness.

"We shouldn't have." Kammi uses "we" and speaks for both of us. She takes the blame when I'm the one who talked her into going. Kammi is like that.

"You're both all right. That's what matters." Mother says "both" but she looks right at me, looks at me in a way she hasn't for the past year. It's the most she's said since Dr. Bindas delivered us back to *Blauwe Huis*.

I open my mouth to say yes or something, but nothing comes out. Instead, I nod.

"I'll let you rest," she says. "Maybe, Kammi, you'll come with me. I see you're reading the article on color theory. I can show you more about that."

Before Mother even finishes speaking, Kammi has scooted off the bed and out the door. Mother closes the door behind her, and I hear it click softly. I close my eyes and let my bones sink into sleep.

The next day, I'm up again.

When I hear Mother in the kitchen with Martia, I dare to sneak upstairs into the inner sanctum. Bolder than ever, I have to see the painting. It's still there, protected from view, but this time I can tell it's closer to being finished. It's not just the blue boat now; there are figures seated in it. Two people, I'm not sure who, but one is a man and one a woman. The faces are turned away at an angle, as if the artist can't quite make them out herself. Could it be Mother in the boat with Dad? Is she painting herself into the scene a year too late? Is she trying to get it right? To forgive and be forgiven? The strokes of paint depicting each person are choppy and layered, standing out almost in relief. I could reach out and touch the people, feel them in three dimensions. I could leave a fingerprint. Evidence.

The teakettle whistles, and I hear voices. Downstairs but close. Mother and Mrs. Bindas. Mrs. Bindas is apologizing for Mayur's behavior, for all the boys. I hear the pain in her voice.

"Mayur, he is most embarrassed," Mrs. Bindas says. "For not taking better care of his guests."

Is he embarrassed about what he did with me? What I let him do?

Teacups clink on a tray. Through the slit in the slightly open door, I peek down the metal staircase. I catch the glitter of a bangled wrist. Mrs. Bindas. Martia moves in front of her, pours tea for her and Mother. They start talking, with Mrs. Bindas speaking first, asking about how I am after the "accident." She shakes her head as Mother tells her I'm fine. Mrs. Bindas says, "Oh, that is good. After all that has happened, she is getting better." Mrs. Bindas doesn't mean my fall. "And Kammi is a delight. She is good for Cyan."

Kammi good for me? I slip out the French doors onto the widow's walk. I can't be seen from where they sit below. They'd have to walk out onto the deck and look up to know I'm here.

A creak sounds behind me. I spin around.

Not Mother. Kammi. Mother's voice still murmurs below, saying all the right things to Mrs. Bindas. How she appreciates the picnic, how it was not the Bindases' fault, what happened at the cave.

"What are you doing up here?" I say in a whisper.

"Same as you." Kammi tiptoes closer, peers over my arm to see below. She grins. Living dangerously. "I knew you came up here," she says when I don't answer.

I shrug.

Kammi tiptoes over to the painting. She turns to face it. I watch her eyes. They widen when she sees the figures in the boat. She looks at me.

I nod. I know.

I turn back to look downstairs. Martia offers refills and a plate of her cookies. As she stirs sugar into her tea, Mrs. Bindas says, "I would love to see some of your paintings."

Mother sits on the couch, just out of sight. She laughs a little. "As I said before, I come here mostly to relax." Another lie. Mother has practice.

"You are too modest," Mrs. Bindas says. "I read about your exhibits in New York, Atlanta."

At the mention of Atlanta, Kammi and I share a look. Atlanta is the tie between us.

"It must be very nice to be so talented. To have so much freedom." Mrs. Bindas sips tea.

Mother doesn't answer. Mrs. Bindas hasn't asked a question. What do freedom and talent have to do with each other?

"Perhaps just a little one, to see," Mrs. Bindas says. "To say I have seen the famous artist's work. The one you will bring to our party."

"Not yet," Mother says. "I don't like to show my work before it's finished."

Mrs. Bindas sighs. "I was afraid you would say no. How about to see your studio? I would like that very much."

"Oh," Mother laughs. "It's messy. In the middle of things. Paints and brushes everywhere."

"Is okay. I should like to see. Very much."

Will Mother bring Mrs. Bindas up to her studio? She's never let anyone up here.

"Well," Mother says. She stands and walks toward the spiral staircase. Her footstep sounds on the first step, her heel striking the metal like a gong.

I grab Kammi's arm and point to the roof. She nods, her eyes large. I motion for her to take off her slides. The soles will make too much noise.

I can't help myself, though. Even as I hear Mrs. Bindas following Mother up the thirteen steps, I want to stay and listen.

"Dr. Bindas said he might make a studio for me," she says.

The sea and the wind whip Mother's response away. But even as Mrs. Bindas talks, I can feel Mother tightening inside. "When people ask about artists," Mother said once to Philippa, not to me, though I overheard as they worked in Mother's studio at home, "it isn't about the artist, it's about the person asking the question. It's about that person's hopes and dreams and the creation of their other self." Mother hates that, people's false interest.

Holding Kammi's hand, I lead her around the narrow ledge. I learned this escape route one summer. It was dangerous then, the metal balustrades rusty in the salt air. Now I'm sore from the fall. As we slip out of view from the widow's walk, I hear Mother at the French doors, blaming Martia for leaving the door unlatched, complaining to Mrs. Bindas about how hard it is to get help who understands an artist's needs, who doesn't insert herself in family matters, and who knows her place. But, she says, Martia is comfortable, like an old aunt.

"We have to slide along here . . . there's a small ledge," I say to Kammi. "Just grip the edge of the roof and slide."

Kammi stares at me.

"Don't worry. I've done it before. Just don't look down." It's funny. After the fall in the cave, I should be afraid. I'm not, though. Here I can see. I can breathe.

I ease my way along the ledge, sliding my hands along the overhanging cupola roofline above me. In another ten feet, the house is closer to the ground, seemingly carved into the earth, like a ship run aground into a beachhead. I jump, landing on the shell drive in my flip-flops. Every muscle shrieks.

When I can speak again, I say, "Your turn." I motion Kammi down. She balances herself, slipping into her shoes. She pauses, suspended, and then jumps. She gasps when she lands.

The kitchen curtain flickers. Martia pulls it back to see what's happening.

"Come on," I say, and we head off down the beach. Martia won't have to lie to Mother and say she hasn't seen us.

CHAPTER TWENTY-SEVEN

THE DAY before Kammi leaves, Mother allows her-self to be the center of attention at Mrs. Bindas's party. Instead of accepting Mrs. Bindas's offer to send a driver, Mother hires Jinco to take us the short distance in his taxi. Mother holds her canvas, still mounted to the easel, not trusting it to Jinco since it's painted in oils and still wet. For once, he doesn't spit shells out from under his tires as we leave. Kammi carries a canvas, too. It's smaller and com-pletely covered. Since it's a watercolor, unlike Mother's, it's safely dry.

Mrs. Bindas opens the door herself, before we knock.

"Ah, we are so happy. Please to come in," she says.

I wonder about Mayur, whether he will attend.

"Is Dr. Bindas coming?" I ask instead.

"No, no, only women are allowed to stay today," Mrs. Bindas says, smiling. "All the boys, they are out of the house."

Kammi's face droops—she was hoping to see Saco. I thought I'd be relieved not to see Mayur, but I'm not sure. I wonder if he's told the other boys he touched me, if they've laughed about the easy American girl.

Mrs. Bindas is all happiness as we follow her inside. "Come, come. Bring your work." She motions Mother in with her easel. "You, too, Kammi," she adds as Kammi offers her own watercolor.

"The oil paint is still wet." Mother maneuvers her canvas carefully. She sets up her easel in the center of the room, a place of honor. Other empty easels stand around the perimeter of the room to hold guests' work. Nothing, though, will be allowed to overshadow Mother's.

I see Mother's completed painting for the first time. Even without the ultramarine paint tube I never returned, she has managed to evoke the sea. A mixed-color wake trails the blue boat as it cuts through the water, moving away from the artist. I imagine that Mother painted the boat with an invisible bridge of good fortune overhead, framing it, like Philippa's painting of the Bridge of Sighs. The figures in the boat are still muted, shadowed, as if not real but imagined. The way Mother and I would have wanted the scene to be. I can now make out three people: a man, a woman, and, I think, a child.

"Striking," Mrs. Bindas says, as if she read that comment

in an art magazine. As if she doesn't trust herself to speak about the painting, especially considering the subject. The blue boat. The name *The Nautilus* is even painted ever so faintly on the side. It can be seen only if one knows to look for it.

"Right here, Kammi." Mrs. Bindas directs her to place her smaller watercolor of the island and the sea from the day of our hike to Mount Christoffel.

"And what have you worked with Kammi on?" Mrs. Bindas asks Mother. "She is such a lucky girl."

"I haven't even seen this piece, and Kammi refused to show it to me in advance." Mother sounds stern, but it's hard to tell what she's really thinking.

Kammi unwraps the painting and clips it to the easel. She grins and steps back so that Mother and Mrs. Bindas can see it in the clear light coming through the window.

Mother doesn't react at first. I'm used to this, but Kammi starts shifting from one foot to the other, like a little kid.

Now that she's finished her seascape, I see that Kammi really does have talent. Whether it would match Catrione's or Philippa's, or whether Mother will ever take on another student, even a stepdaughter-to-be, is hard to tell.

"Who helped you with this?" Mother asks, walking back and forth in front of the painting to catch the best light. To see the strokes, to study the color blends Kammi used.

Kammi looks at me before she answers. "Cyan."

Mother's gaze goes from Kammi's face to mine and back to the painting. "Cyan?"

"Yes, she helped me focus, to see all the colors."

Mother nods and stares at the painting, as if deciphering how Kammi captured the glints of light on the water, how much is Kammi's work and how much mine.

"It's good. A study in contrast."

For Mother, that is high praise. Kammi beams.

Mrs. Bindas pats me on the arm, as if she's known all along I have an artist's soul, and then she flits away to greet her friends.

I take that chance to snag a cold drink and some finger food. A chicken wrap, with some exotic sauce oozing out the wrapper bottom. An odd-looking green, but edible.

When they come into the room, Mrs. Bindas's guests approach Mother with awe, standing close to her but not daring to make eye contact or say anything to her. Then they wander away to study Mother's painting in depth or to size up the competition for gallery space.

Mother walks over to stand by me. For once, she doesn't say anything about the amount of food I've taken from the buffet. She looks out at the crowd, smiling and nodding at people as they catch her eye. Her public face. "What's Kammi talking about, you helping?"

"You didn't think I could?" I answer Mother's question with my own.

"I didn't say that. I didn't think you wanted to enough."

"Enough to what?" That's what I've always wondered.

"Enough to give art everything you had—and then more. To give up love." Mother swirls a slice of lemon in her sparkling water. This time without alcohol.

"Is that what you did?"

"Yes. My mother had this notion that painting was only for children. Adult women had to give up certain things to be successful in other, more important areas of our lives. She said that the life of an artist was a selfish way to live."

I look at Mother, puzzled. Her mother, my grandmother Betts, plied me with paints when I was very small. Mother was the one who discouraged me. Grandmother always said I could be anything I wanted.

"Your grandmother mellowed with age," Mother says, as if reading the protest forming in my mind. "But to me, that's what she said. Every day of my childhood, practically."

"So why repeat that?" I ask. "When you didn't believe it?"

"Because what my mother said and did made me tougher. I was tough enough to deal with not having enough money early on to pay my bills."

Mother walks around Kammi's painting again. "Not bad," she says.

"That means great, right?" I ask.

Mother nods. "For a first-timer. Guess she had a tube of ultramarine?"

I feel myself blush, something I rarely do anymore.

"And what about Philippa?" I ask, my voice low.

Mother stands still next to me, almost as if she hasn't heard me. As if she's heard a memory whispering.

"Mayur told me there was a note," I say. "From Pippa. To Dad."

Mother stiffens. Maybe she's going to lie to me. She sips from her glass and sighs. "Was that what happened on the hiking trip?" She turns to me. "I thought Mayur was up to no good."

I nod. "Mayur said it was a love letter."

Mother holds out her hand, as if steadying the easel holding Kammi's painting.

"Yes" is all she says.

"That day . . . the day Dad went out in the boat. Did you know about the letter?"

She shakes her head. The air goes out of me. "Not the letter."

"Then why didn't you go?" I wonder if she revises the trip over and over in her mind like I do. Whether, in the new version, she says yes.

"Your father and I had drifted apart. He'd come back to reconcile, he said. I wasn't ready. At first, I didn't know about Philippa. But your father told me she'd seen him in Italy. Looked him up. *Been* with him. *Pippa.* I should have seen it coming." Mother seems far away from me.

She doesn't ask me about the note, what it said, whether Mayur gave it to me. I remember the words about there being only a single color in the world—not blue, not yellow, not pink. Only the color of love. I don't tell her that I held the note for a moment in my hand, that I lost it in the cave at Mount Christoffel. Maybe someday.

"Why'd she send the postcard?" I ask. The Bridge of Sighs, for lovers.

"I think it's a kind of apology." Mother's voice is soft, softer than I ever hear it. I almost don't breathe, because this is like a magic spell that will break if I talk too loudly, if I ask another question. If a cloud moves in front of the sun.

If it was an apology, did Mother accept it? Would I?

When the last guest leaves, Mother collapses her easel, keeping the canvas clipped to it to transport it back to Maine.

"You'll exhibit this in New York?" Mrs. Bindas asks.

"Not right away," Mother says. She needs time to let the paint dry.

The door opens, and Dr. Bindas appears.

"Oh, so sorry," he says. "I thought the party was over." He starts to back out, shooing boys behind him. I see Saco and then Mayur peer around him. Kammi smiles at Saco, who grins and lets himself be pulled back. Mayur smirks from behind his father's shoulder, then looks to make sure the others haven't noticed. He hasn't told them, I'm sure. There is now another secret between us. But this one we share. I roll my eyes at him and he disappears behind his father.

"No, Dr. Bindas, please to come in and say goodbye to Mrs. Walters," Mrs. Bindas calls after him. Dr. Bindas, stiff in his short-sleeved shirt and pressed slacks, enters and nods to my mother. Very proper. His physician's eyes then take me in. He sees I'm no worse for wear, the bruises fading from blue to yellow.

"Glad to see you are feeling better," he says.

"Thank you."

Kammi raises an eyebrow, motioning toward the door. I shake my head at her. I'm not interested in Mayur. Absolutely not. Maybe.

"We are indebted to you," Mother says.

Dr. Bindas raises a hand. "No, it was so little, and we are grateful. No permanent injuries. Here, let me help you. We shall drive you back."

Dr. Bindas reaches to take Mother's painting. Mother's never let anyone else handle a fresh painting.

"No," I say, suddenly not wanting anyone else to touch *The Blue Boat*.

"It's all right, Cyan," Mother says, touching my arm. "Dr. Bindas, wet canvases require special handling. I'd feel better carrying it myself."

Dr. Bindas blushes, as if he's done something improper, but he nods politely, as always. He holds the door for Mother.

Even when she moves away to allow Mrs. Bindas to hug her ever so gently before we leave, the warmth from Mother's touch on my skin lingers.

"Do you want to go to the airport?" Mother asks me the next morning. As I did the day Kammi arrived, I shake my head. It's only been a few weeks since then, and yet it seems like months. Time is like that. Fast and yet slow, like waves of light shimmering through glass. Goethe said that, in order to be seen, every color must have light within it or behind it. Blue is the first color that appears when darkness is penetrated by light.

Mother doesn't ask a second time. She slips into the cab. From the window closest to me, Kammi waves. Excited like a kid going home from summer camp, she moves her arm back and forth in a wide arc. The top edge of her carefully wrapped painting peeks over the back seat.

I hold my hand up in the air, not waving. But I imagine my hand touching hers through the air, the glass. My yellow to her pink. I don't think about Howard yet. He's overeager, like the puppy he gave to Kammi's mother. But he might be okay.

Jinco pulls away, bits of shell spitting from under his tires. If he's watching Kammi through the rearview mirror, he'll be subtle so Mother doesn't see him. She wouldn't like it. Kammi won't notice, either. Later, I'll tell her, warn her about guys.

Martia stands next to me, but she doesn't put her arm around my waist or hug me. I don't have to say I'm okay. Martia knows somehow, knows I don't want to be too close. She steps inside, and the scent of food wafts through the open door. For once, I am not ravenous.

Tonight, before Mother and I finish packing, Martia will go home to her family. To her children and mother. They must already be thinking of the sweet *kokada* treats she'll bring.

In my room, I open the box of sea glass and add the photo of Martia's family to it. Then I get out the largest, bluest piece I have, the one I keep in the sock, and hold it to the light. Without my jeweler's pliers, I use my hands to pull the wire I've hidden away straight. The sterling silver grows warm in my hand. It curves around my finger and over the glass. I wrap until the silver holds the glass fast, and I twist it to make a loop, securing the back of the glass. I file the rough edge before tucking it underneath. Hiding it.

In the bottom of the box, there's still the sliver of sharp, clear glass from the blue boat. If I toss it back into the sea, years from now the ocean will have worn down the jagged edges. Someday, the sea will give up its smooth treasure along the shore for someone else to find.

Maybe my box is like the one Pandora decided to open. Maybe I was too curious, like she was. But with all the chaos and longing, everything Pandora released into the world, there was something else at the bottom of the box, a gift.

Hope.

I think that's what we have left, Mother and me. I give it to both of us, cupping it in my hands like a piece of tumbled sea glass, holding it up to the light.

ACKNOWLEDGMENTS

Thank you to the Society of Children's Book Writers and Illustrators (SCBWI) for years of community and a Work-in-Progress grant for an earlier, unpublished novel.

Thanks to Lisa Fraustino, Han Nolan, Alexandria LaFaye, and Amanda Cockrell of Hollins University's Graduate Program in Children's Literature for gentle encouragement and the occasional kick in the rear. To Hollins students Brie Shannon, Candice Ransom, Tere Stouffer, Amie Rotruck, the Owl Girls, and the Wildflour online group—thank you for your friendship.

With appreciation to the Writer's Center of Bethesda, Maryland, and its committee, Northern Virginia Writers, for bringing writing to the larger Washington, D.C., community through such gifted instructors as Barbara Esstman.

Thanks to Lee Smith and the members of her Advanced Fiction Workshop at the Key West Literary Seminar, January 2008.

For the Rector Lane Irregulars—Donna, Carla, Ellen, Peggy, Laura, Noreen, and Sandi—thank you for a roundtable of mystery and sisterly support.

Thanks to Leone Ciporin, Marcy Dolan, Lee Lawrence, and Sue Buck for believing.

With special thanks to my children's writing group—Ellen Braaf, Erin Teagan, Sydney Dunlap, Lorrie-Ann Melnick, and Corinne Wetzel. To Ellen, who does so much for the Mid-Atlantic SCBWI and for the Writer's Center and who still has more love for others and their dreams than anyone I know, an extra hug.

For the wonderful agent and literary godmother Sarah Davies of the Greenhouse Literary Agency—thank you so much for helping me realize a dream.

With special thanks to editor Jennifer Wingertzahn for loving Cyan from the beginning and for guiding me along with a gentle touch and a kind soul. And to everyone else at Clarion Books, thank you for making *The Other Side of Blue* such a beautiful book.

Thank you to my parents and late grandmother for encouraging my love of books; to my siblings, Melanie and John, for letting me subject them to my earliest writing efforts; and, to my sister-in-law Jane for artistic consultation—any errors are my own.

To Tom, who has never wavered in his support of my dreams despite too many takeout dinners and a seriously cluttered desk, thank you for being on the journey with me.